D1267979

world of nothing

Books by Ronald L. Fair

World of Nothing

Hog Butcher

Many Thousand Gone

world of nothing

two novellas

by ronald l. fair

Harper & Row, Publishers
New York, Evanston, and London

The author wishes to acknowledge his gratitude to the Center for Advanced Studies and to its Director, Dr. Philip P. Hallie, at Wesleyan University, where, as a Visiting Fellow in 1969, Mr. Fair completed this book.

 For information address Harper & Row, Publishers, Inc., 49 East 33rd Street, New York, N.Y. 10016. Published simultaneously in Canada by Fitzhenry & Whiteside Limited, Toronto.

FIRST EDITION

LIBRARY OF CONGRESS CATALOG CARD NUMBER: 71-105237

For Sterling Brown

contents

Where is this Heaven
That one goes to after death?
Perhaps it is here.

Where is this place Hell
Where bodies are said to burn?
Perhaps it is here.

jerome

prologue

It was said by the old woman who lived in the attic of the frame house at the end of the block that Jerome had been blessed by more than one god.

Since the day his young mother returned from the county hospital with the child so warmly wrapped in a bunting the hospital had provided for her, the old lady had been encouraged by those strange forces she knew so well to visit the child. The powers confronting her were stronger than any she had known, and although she did not quite know how, she knew they were different.

She was frightened of them. She had resisted the influences that were forcing her to the child by every means she knew, and then finally by potions other mediums had given her and words they had said to counteract what they felt surely must be a spell someone of great power had cast upon her—perhaps even the devil. But the combined abilities of these ladies could not defeat this tremendous power, and so she went to visit this strange little round-faced boy, knowing that if she resisted any longer she would anger a force that she could not combat, thereby endangering her own life.

Jerome's mother and grandmother had been to the old woman's apartment on occasion to aid them in their search for the right number to play that day, or for the cure for a coughing spell that had come over the boy's grandmother and lasted for six months while the doctors at the county hospital examined and reexamined her chest, only to find, each time, that there was nothing wrong with her. The old woman recognized the coughing spell at once as the work of a voodooist and counteracted it with long ceremonial chanting and herbs mailed to her from a friend in Louisiana.

She had always been welcome in the apartment, and it was no surprise when she appeared at the door with a pot of her special stew, dressed in her customary black dress and coat. No one had ever seen her wear anything but this long black dress that turned under only slightly above her ankles.

When she entered the apartment, she felt the presence of powers stronger than any she had known in her long life, and she was frightened by them. But she suppressed her fears, not wanting to alarm the others, and the three women talked quietly of happenings in the neighborhood while they waited for the child Jerome to awaken for his feeding.

Jerome's mother, Lula, felt slightly unnerved that this woman whom she called a witch had expressed so much interest in her son. It was true that she had told her in only the second month of her pregnancy that the child would be a boy, but Lula was still afraid to show him to her. However, she was also fearful that something tragic might happen if she did not, so when Jerome awakened, she dutifully went to the bed, took him into her arms, holding him tightly against her breasts, and, trembling from fear, walked into the living room to show her son to the old woman, praying to God (the God she knew) all the time that the witch would not by her presence cast a spell of evil over her son.

As she entered the room, the old woman spoke. "Ain't no need for you to be afraid of me, child. I ain't gonna do him no harm. I can't harm anybody that special. I came here cause I couldn't stay away no longer. God knows I tried. I ain't gonna hurt him, but if I don't see him somethin' terrible's gonna happen to me."

Lula heard very little of what the old woman said. Indeed, she was so terrified of her that she had not understood anything she had said. Slowly, painfully she turned back the blanket from his face and Jerome turned his tiny head and looked at the witch.

The old woman looked into his eyes and he into hers. They remained this way for some time, the old woman appearing to be in one of her trances, the child looking innocently at her—but looking. Then a smile came over the witch's face, and she sat back in her seat and sighed heavily.

Lula began feeding him, the contentment of a mother nursing her child all about her. So content was she that she did not notice Jerome's eyes turning repeatedly toward the old woman.

When Lula had finished feeding Jerome and put him back to bed, the old woman said words over the house, blessing it in the strange manner she knew. As she was leaving, she said, "I don't know who's done it, but that boy's been blessed by god—by what I would call a different god."

Lula and her mother watched the old witch as she

hurried through the snow on her way not to her dark attic dwelling, but to the apartment of someone else in the neighborhood who was in need of her powers of healing, and wondered what she had meant by her departing remark.

Surely she was not saying there was more than one God. There was the devil. They knew that. And there was God. There was God the Father, God the Son and God the Holy Ghost; but that was all one God, and knowing her as they did, they knew that she also believed thus. Of course there was the devil, but even though they knew the old woman believed in his existence, they felt she surely had not come to accept the devil as a god.

Jerome's grandmother was confused, but not really worried. She knew that the old woman often spoke in strange ways. Lula, however, was tormented by her words. "But, Momma," she protested, "there's only one God. And if Jerome's been blessed by someone else, it must be by the devil."

It had been one full week since the old lady had visited them, saying that Jerome was blessed by a different god, and Lula was still troubled by these words. Again tonight, as she lay in bed with Jerome held closely to her as if she were protecting him from her younger brothers and sisters who shared the bed with her, she found it difficult to sleep. Ever since "the night of the witch," as Lula called it, she had been troubled by evil spirits. She would stare at the ceiling until it came alive with misshapen creatures, all smelling of evil. And then, after she had brought them into focus, she would watch in horror as they went through their ritual of destroying people and each other.

They were indeed devils. She knew they were devils. And they were not in her mind. They were real, alive, and they were performing their cruelties against the dead spirits of men and women in her room. But why had they chosen her room? When they appeared, everything smelled of death and dripped blood. Perhaps they had not brought their evil to her room to torture her, but only to invite her to join their world.

She looked at Jerome, reminding herself that none of this had happened until she brought him home from the hospital to this room, and wondered if perhaps he had indeed been blessed by the devil.

But how could it be possible? She had seen these same devils in dreams when she was younger, but the church had chased them away from her. Still, she was terrified that someday they would return to her life, but as *real* people. And if they ever returned, she had felt certain they would be after her.

Lula watched them go through their acts with all the fury and intensity of madmen. Now she focused on one and watched him bite off a woman's head. Blood dripped from his mouth as he discarded the headless carcass and snatched up another woman, running all the time so that he knocked other people down and trampled them to death as his feet crushed them, ripped the arm off the new woman and forced her to watch him as he ate it, and then, slowly, he inserted her head into his mouth and bit it off with his teeth. It seemed to Lula that the screams continued even while the devil was chewing the head. And over the screams she could hear the noise of the woman's skull cracking as he chewed.

"God help me," Lula whispered. But how could God come to her aid now that she was no longer deserving of his help? It had been years since the monsters had visited her, and she was fascinated by their ugliness and by the ease with which they destroyed the weaker, defenseless human beings. She was particularly attracted to one small monster, the size of a mere child, who could expand his tiny mouth so wide that he could swallow a human being three times his size. "God help me. God help me," she pleaded.

He had helped her once before. He had been good to her once before. Maybe he would return to her life and free her from these monsters. The Episcopal priest, Father Jennings, had helped chase them away from her mind by his soft words and knowledgeable counsel. She was only ten when she started going to him. Her girl friends had all left the Baptist church that year when the handsome young curate came to Saint Luke's Church. Surely God was not punishing her because she had left her own church and gone to this new one? No. He could not have done it for that reason, but he could have done it for other reasons.

She was thirteen before Father Jennings was able to persuade her to go to confession. All the other girls went that year. There were at least fifteen of them, the year she was confirmed, and Father Jennings had told them that confession was necessary for their souls.

They all confessed one thing in common: that they had come to his church only because he was there and they were infatuated with him. He had come into Lula's drab world of almost nothing and brought along with him ideas for entertainment, for activities, for fun! There were dances every Friday night in the basement of the church. There were picnics and outings to places she could not possibly have seen had she not been a member of the church. She had even been able to go away to summer camp.

She was so happy that summer of her thirteenth birthday. She was able to get away from her six sisters and brothers and be alone in the woods in Wisconsin. The boys from a nearby camp came over every night, two or three at a time, and every night, after Father Jennings and the counselors had gone to sleep, Lula would go to bed with another one of the young boys, and sometimes with several in one night. But that was only the first week of camp. The boys left after that, and she was tormented by her sins. There was only one thing she could think of doing to cleanse herself.

So she went to Father Jennings' cabin late one night to confess her sins to God and ask for forgiveness. She confessed and, as usual, her emotions exploded into compulsive, almost hysterical crying. Father Jennings embraced her comfortingly, but she would not stop crying. Finally, he took her face in his hands and kissed her tenderly on the mouth and she erupted with all the passion of a mature woman.

After that she slept with Father Jennings nightly, and although originally she was supposed to stay in camp only one more week, he arranged to have her appointed to the staff and she remained for another month.

She had become his woman. On Sundays when he said mass and preached his sermons about evil and the devil and fallen man, she smiled proudly, overjoyed that her man was not only a good lover, but was also such a dynamic preacher. That could have been the sin. She loved him. She loved him more than God. That could have been the sin that had brought out those masses of creatures that tormented her nightly.

When she discovered she was pregnant she went to Father Jennings and he suggested that she have an abortion. She was afraid. She said she wanted to have his baby and that he should marry her because it was his child and because it was the only Christian thing for him to do. That was perhaps another sin.

He told her he felt the child could not possibly be his; that her confession had proved to him that it could have been fathered by any number of young men. Lula pleaded that it had been different with him, that she felt love for him and felt that she wanted to give him a child, and *that* surely must have been the reason for her pregnancy. Women couldn't get pregnant unless they wanted to, she argued.

He laughed at her, saying, "You're a damn whore. Oh, you're a young one all right, but you're still a whore."

Lula felt he was probably right. And if he was, if she was a whore, then that was another sin. There were several sins. Many sins. And perhaps the greatest sin was the sin of being glad to be away from her six brothers and sisters, of feeling special because she had been freed from their roach- and rodent-infested, crowded, smelly apartment that summer. She was proud that God had chosen her and she was proud that this summer she was freed from the filth of the tiny three-room apartment and the unpleasantness of her family; she felt that she was better than all of them.

And then she had been made an employee of the camp—and at only thirteen, too—and she knew she was even better than the other girls from the neighborhood, who were jealous of her; better than all of them because they all wanted to sleep with him and she had done it. She had become his woman. Even far into her pregnancy she was still his woman. She controlled him. She owned him. She had even forced him to make love to her in the church. Right on the altar! In front of God. That, too, had been a sin that might have caused God to turn away from her. But at that time she did not care. He was hers. She took her young body to him regularly and tightened her control.

And then one day she heard that he was to be married. He was marrying a young woman considerably older than Lula; one who was returning from college, who had come from a *good* family and had money. So she took her body, full of life, to him again. This time, however, he rejected her, saying no, not this close to his wedding day.

She started to leave and he patted her, saying, "If you've had that baby when I get back from my honeymoon, come by and see me."

"Fuck you, Father," she said angrily. "Do you hear me? Fuck you!"

He smiled and whispered, "That's exactly what I mean." He put his hands on her shoulders, saying, "Now don't be such a little bitch. You know you'll be back to me. You have to come to me."

And that was still another sin, because she wanted him right then, and had indeed returned several times since the birth of Jerome.

But that day she was determined not to leave until he had made love to her. She had given herself to him whenever he asked for her, and now she wanted him to join with her this last time before he went away with the other woman. She had seen the woman he was to marry often when she had come to mass. As much as Lula disliked her, she had to admit that she was pretty. But even so, Lula felt she was much too fragile for Father Jennings. "Hell," she had said to one of her girl friends, "she ain't got no ass at all." How could he enjoy someone so skinny, she had asked herself repeatedly. How can she be his woman when she's not even as big as I am?

Lula began folding vestments as she continued arguing with him, but now she lowered her voice and began crying softly. She bent over to place the neatly folded vestments in a lower drawer and felt his eyes on her. Knowing just how he was watching her, she remained in that position, busying herself by rearranging things in the drawer. Soon she heard the latch on the door and she smiled and waited. In a few moments she could hear his heavy breathing, and then his hands were on her. He mumbled something to her, she sobbed an incoherent reply, and then she felt him entering her body, and as her head swirled she heard him at the altar saying, "Take. Eat. This is my body which is given for you. Do this in remembrance of me." There in the sacristy where the holy wine and holy bread and holy water were kept, where those symbols of God remained locked up until they were miraculously transformed into the actual body and blood of Jesus Christ, there where God was to be safe from the sins of man, her mind floated in the joy of his entering her body.

Lula closed her eyes and the devils on the ceiling dissolved into many colors, spinning faster until they transformed themselves into screams. She let out a slight whimper, caught herself, not wanting to wake the baby, and then, after looking at him, pushed him away from her. He *was* evil, she thought. She knew he was evil. He was her son, but he was also a devil. God had really blessed her in a strange way, she thought. "God damn you, God," she whispered into the darkness, and the little devils came out on the ceiling and began dancing and promising her treasures.

Now she looked at Jerome differently. This was the first time the devils had done anything like this. Could he really be a devil? Could he be their king? Well, after all, treasures, devils, her son . . . She smiled and took him back into her arms. Then she remembered that everything about his birth had been different. Father Jennings had been unable to take her to the hospital because he was out of town with his new wife. Her mother's boyfriend was either working or drunk somewhere. He was always working or drunk somewhere, she had said to her younger brothers and sisters.

Or, if he was there, he was in bed with her mother, waking all of them up either because they were fighting or because of the noise he made when they made love. But when he wasn't drunk or making love or fighting, he was working somewhere, long, hard hours, even though he never had anything to show for it. Lula could not understand why a man who worked so many hours a day made so little money. To her a coal hiker should have made as much money as anyone else, and she did not understand that such was not the way life treated some people, that he did not even make a living wage on that job, so he had two others and that left him at home very little, and very anxious for his woman when he was there.

Her mother obviously could not take her. How could she leave the six younger children? But she gave her more than enough money for cab fare and sent her off, telling her that she would be along as soon as the old woman came to watch after the children. Her mother, however, did not visit her at the hospital until four days later. But never once did Lula experience anything that she considered to be real pain, and never once was she afraid. Now that she thought about it, she had not been afraid of anything since the day of Jerome's birth; at least not anything human, or anything other than the monsters.

Even during the many hours she was in labor, although she was almost completely out of her head from panting and from the contractions, there seemed to be a kind of soothing music in her head. And when they brought Jerome to her, he seemed to sparkle like a precious black stone, and there was always the feeling of something different when the nurses entered the room with him. She could not identify it—it was just something different and special. And when she left the hospital, the nurses all kissed Jerome good-bye. He was indeed special.

Lula held him close to her and thought: If he's my special devil then I'll make the most of him, and the creatures appeared again and danced more for her.

Lula's life had become quite different. Years before, she would have felt that God had performed some miracle to alter the ugliness of her existence, but now she accepted the change as something brought about by Jerome. After all, the creatures had told her she would begin to enjoy pleasures heretofore unknown to her. And they had not lied. She felt the point of change was from the moment she openly accepted Jerome as the son of the devil. That surely was the action that made them scream and dance so furiously. The very next day the state welfare department honored her with a check in her name so that she might support herself and Jerome. And even though her mother's name was also on the check, she was delighted with the knowledge that this was the beginning of those good times she had been promised by the creatures.

Less than a week later, the elderly woman who had cooked the late Saturday night dinners and Sunday afternoon brunches for the parishioners for so many years decided that she was too old to stand at the hot stoves any longer, and retired. Immediately, the women of the rector's guild decided to offer the position to Lula, with pay. They felt they were helping her to improve her life. Lula accepted, although she had never enjoyed the idea of being a cook or a servant, feeling that the position was only temporary.

The first few meals she prepared were much too heavily seasoned for the sophisticated palates of those ladies a few steps above her lowly position in life, but the biscuits for the Sunday afternoon brunch delighted them so that they were willing to work with her, lightening the Southern-influenced, heavy-pepper hand, until her meals were almost as bland as theirs.

They were doing good things for Lula, they told themselves in their smug self-righteousness. They were helping her to find a new life. They had done a very strange thing indeed. They had accepted not only this bastard child, but also her bastard, and made them both, truly, a living part of their religious community.

They were so fascinated by Jerome's enormous eyes and the warmth of his presence that they were only too happy to care for him, oftentimes without even being asked. For many of the guild members, even though their reasons were wrong, this was the first time they were practicing the Christianity they had talked of for so many years. They were good ladies. They were being kind to someone they considered beneath them. Where Jerome was concerned, they were overflowing with the goodness of Christianity. The rector, Father Walker, was finally able to say that he was proud of them; that now they were living the true Christlike existence.

The following year Father Jennings' wife, Marlene, began to radiate a warmth that had not been present in her face before, and the congregation waited anxiously for her to tell them of her pregnancy.

Lula was the first to know, for she and Marlene, working closely together on so many activities in the church over the past year, had become devoted friends. Lula, sworn to secrecy, did not tell the others, but she was afraid for her own well-being, feeling that perhaps a baby would change Father Jennings so that he would turn away from her. It was true that externally she and Marlene really were friends, but Lula hated the fact that Marlene was going to have his baby. She wished that something could be done to prevent it.

The ladies of the church had for a long time been impressed with the gentle Marlene, and when she told them of her pregnancy they decided that she should have permanent help in her house. After all, even though Father Jennings was only a curate, his wife was surely deserving of a servant, especially at this time in her life, and what better person to help her than the mother of Jerome.

When they approached Marlene with their plan, she was moved to tears because it meant that she would no longer be alone on those nights when Father Jennings was visiting the sick in hospitals and taking communion to the shut-ins. Now she would have her friend Lula with her at all times. They would become a new family, and Jerome, also, would at last have a father figure in his presence. Marlene embraced Lula, telling her how wonderful it would be now that they were all going to live together.

Lula said, "Thank you," modestly, suppressing the extreme joy she felt at being able to live in the same house with her lover. That night the devils danced on the ceiling of her bedroom as usual, only this night she asked them questions about her future, and although they did not answer in any language that she could understand, she was certain that their actions indicated that someday Father Jennings would be her man alone.

When Marlene told Father Jennings about the decision of the ladies of the church, he was as she had never seen him before. "No," he shouted. "I don't want that little tramp living under the same roof with my family. You have no idea what that girl's capable of doing."

Marlene replied patiently, "I hope you're not allowing yourself to be influenced by things she may have told you in the confessional. If you are," she said, considerably firmer, "may God help you."

"No, it's nothing like that. It's just—"

"Besides, the ladies in three guilds have pledged to raise funds for her salary. It won't come out of the church treasury, so Father Walker can't possibly object."

"Well," he said after a pause, "if it's what the congregation wants, there's nothing we can do about it except be gracious enough to allow them to help us."

The year before, the ladies of two guilds had raised enough money to buy him a car to show how fond they were of him. After all, he was young and handsome by their standards; handsome and exciting to them only because he was so very young and looked even younger. And that evening, after his prayers, Father Jennings allowed himself to think that perhaps they were preparing him to replace the old rector. He knew the rector would not retire for six or eight years, and that he could not possibly stay on as his assistant with his present salary for that length of time—he could not serve under *anyone* for eight years—but perhaps these ladies were trying to arrange for him to move into a different position, one where he and Father Walker shared the duties of the church equally. Perhaps they were telling him with this gift of a servant that he had already been chosen, and that all he had to do was wait for a few years and then take complete control of one of the most powerful parishes in the city.

Then he remonstrated with himself for this sin of pride. Well, why not, he thought. I can run this parish as well as the old fool. I can run this one and several others, for that matter. I could even run the diocese. Why shouldn't I be a bishop?

Although sleep came to him fast that night, it was not very refreshing, because he found himself waking up continually, first going to the toilet to relieve himself, then to the kitchen for a glass of ice water, and then the next time, early in the morning, to the cabinet where he kept his alcohol. After he was back in bed awhile, he realized that his wife had never once stirred. He was pleased to learn that she was such a heavy sleeper. And just before he, too, succumbed to a deep sleep, he realized that Lula's presence in their house would perhaps be even more of a convenience for him than for his wife. And it was.

Lula packed the three wash dresses she had outgrown only the year before and the one extra set of undergarments in a small cardboard box and went to say good-bye to her mother. As she passed the hall closet, she noticed her winter coat and, after examining it disdainfully, she threw it to her younger sister. It was already fall, but she was confident that she would have a fine new coat before it was too cold. Her sister's joy was so great that she wore the coat all day, even though it was like a day of the summer that had just passed.

She had taken Jerome to the church earlier that day, and there he was being entertained by some of the women of the church. All that was left to do was to leave, but her little brothers and sisters wanted to know why she had to leave them. She had cared for them every bit as much as their own mother, and her leaving was a time of sorrow for them. She had told them it was because she had a job, but when they began crying, asking that she take them with her, she screamed, "I don't ever want to see you little dirty bastards again."

When her mother and the children came to visit her

at the Jennings' household, even though she was proud to be able to show them her room on the third floor and Jerome's room next to hers, she discouraged them from returning because she was ashamed of them. To ease her guilt, however, she gave her mother some of Jerome's old clothing for the new baby that would be arriving soon; also, she gave two dresses to the sister next in age to her. Lula was glad to part with the dresses. It was like ending her past, for that was exactly what she intended to do.

The children came to see her once or twice after that, but she made them so uncomfortable that, soon, even though they were so very young, they knew she did not want them there, and they did not return unless it was because they were so very hungry that the pains made them suppress their pride. If she met them on the street, she was cordial, and if someone else was around, perhaps a member of the congregation, she always made it a point to give them a dime or a quarter. But outside of these chance meetings, she rarely saw them. Indeed, once she had seen a little brother coming toward her from the direction of the playground. He had not yet seen her, so she stepped into a doorway until he passed, and then continued on her way, relieved that her foul past had not reached out and licked her fresh, new flesh.

It had all been arranged. The creatures had promised her a new life; she would never be pulled down to those levels of misery and degradation from which she had come. In a weak moment she allowed herself to think that once she had established herself she might be able to help her mother and brothers and sisters, but she dismissed the thought, realizing that by that time they would be able to help themselves, and if they were not . . . well, they would just have to be able to help themselves. The new life had changed her so much that now when she passed an alley and smelled the garbage fermenting there, she was made physically ill because she remembered that her mother's apartment always smelled just as foul as the alleys. She would never return to that existence.

By Jerome's third year on this earth, he had won the love of every member of the parish and also an astonishing degree of respect from persons who had only casual contact with him. He spoke so clearly, using words that no three-year-old should know, and in such an adult way that Father Jennings welcomed his company on trips to the barbershop, visits to the shut-ins, and even on vacations. On the festive outings, Lula, of course, went along. His own child, a girl, had been born so miserably deformed that the doctors released the clamp that had been attached to the umbilical cord, ordered the nurse to leave the room for supplies, and continued working on the mother as the life force flowed out of the child.

The trauma of the "stillborn," as they were told their

child was called, was such that Father Jennings and Marlene had decided not to try to have another child until the memory of the first one was lessened in their minds. Lula's joy over the death of the baby was so great that she actually delighted in waiting on Marlene, pretending sorrow. The child's death had fitted perfectly into Lula's plans. Now that she thought of it, she was certain that she had seen one of the hideous creatures on her ceiling devouring the entrails of a child. She should have known the devils would not let her down. Whatever they promised, they gave, so she pledged her loyalty to them again—to Satan himself. She gave thanks to the devil, to all the devils, on her knees at the foot of Jerome's bed. She would still be important. There would be no new child to replace Jerome and they would each be able to keep their bedroom, rather than her room being turned into a nursery the way Marlene had planned.

She enjoyed waiting on Marlene, spoiling her, because all the while she was laughing at her, laughing because she knew that Marlene had lost and would go on losing all of her life. She would never have a baby by him, never. Her guise worked so well that all the congregation believed that without Lula's help, Marlene might not have recovered from her tragic experience.

After a while, Marlene and Father Jennings began to believe this, too. They would wait before they tried to have another child. There was no rush, they told themselves. After all, they had Jerome, and both he and Lula were almost like their own children now.

And on the day Jerome assumed control of the church

for a few moments Father Jennings was as proud of him as any priest might have been at witnessing his very own son celebrate his first mass. It had been a solemn high mass that day as usual, another priest brought in from the outside to join them, as was their practice, since, although their parish was quite wealthy, the vestry was too miserly to hire another full-time assistant. The recessional had begun, the thurifer filling the scaled-down cathedral-like parish with the mystical smoke of heaven, followed by the ancient choir members singing flat and off key at the full capacity of their lungs, then the acolytes, and finally the three priests, Father Walker coming last, looking as majestic as the Archbishop of Canterbury.

Jerome bowed as the noble figures passed him, then hurried to the altar, where he turned and faced the congregation. "My Father wishes me to speak to you now," he said.

The organist stopped playing because he had the feeling that Jerome's voice had filled the church and drowned him out. The choir also stopped, and when all those within the church were facing him, mouths gaping, Jerome continued: "My Father wishes me to tell you that *all* of you will join his kingdom, but that after death you will have to live again many times before he can see you. He will help you."

Then Jerome returned to his seat and the recessional was concluded.

Had it not been for Marlene embracing him so lovingly, Lula might have beaten him right in the church for what he had done. For although everyone else had been moved by his short sermon, believing that he had in some way been touched by God, she alone felt something else, because while he was on the altar she had seen the devils again. The walls and tapestries came alive with the creatures, and the stations of the cross were so hideously transformed that she almost screamed in agony. She wondered how it could be that all the others were so blind.

Later, downstairs, as she was serving food, she found it difficult to believe that everyone who passed her was really complimenting her for Jerome's performance. Could they all be so blind to what he really is? She asked one of the ladies, "But did you see the church as he spoke?"

"Did I ever," the woman replied enthusiastically. "It was almost as if the clouds were waiting for him to speak before they broke and the sun came pouring onto his face. Why, it was like he was the very sun himself. God has truly blessed you to give you a child like that."

Then she heard them congratulating Father Jennings. "But, Father, how could you teach him so much so fast?"

"He learns fast," Father Jennings said, taking credit for things that had not been of his doing. "Truly an exceptional child with a brilliant mind. I can only hope that someday he'll want to go into the priesthood and serve God to the fullest."

Lula was so confused by what she was seeing: the noise, the compliments, the smell of food, laughter, more praise for Jerome. She felt her body growing weaker and went outside for air. There she saw Jerome playing in the yard with the other children. She thought of going to him, wanting to punish him for what he had done, but as she was about to take the first step toward him, he looked at her and she saw how old, really old, his eyes were. It was as if she were looking into the eyes of an ancient midget, centuries old. And then, as her field of vision widened, she saw not the little boy Jerome, but instead a deformed old man, crippled, face wrinkled, with a long beard. She turned and hurried back into the church, trembling. Jerome continued playing, after having watched his mother hurry back into the basement.

Back inside again, she heard Father Walker, the senior warden and the assistant senior warden complimenting Father Jennings. They all agreed that he had a brilliant career before him. If he could teach Jerome as much as he had taught him in such a short period of time, he would surely have one of the most illustrious careers of any clergyman in recent history. Then the senior warden lowered his voice and began talking about Father Jennings' future with their parish. He said he realized that as only a curate Father Jennings was not receiving much money, but if he would be patient, the vestry would try to get the congregation to raise his salary the following year. "Who knows?" the senior warden said authoritatively. "We may even get another curate to be *your* assistant."

Then Father Walker spoke in his behalf. "Gentlemen, if you had any idea how hard this young man works you wouldn't be talking about raising his salary next year, you would be doing it now."

They agreed that things did not always appear to be just, but that it was coming—they would see justice done toward Father Jennings.

Father Jennings thanked them as humbly as he

could, but his distrust for his superior began working stronger within his mind. So that's his move, he thought. He knows I'm going to take this parish away from him and he wants to hang on so bad that he's willing to become co-rector with me. No one would be able to run my church with me, and no one will run *this* church with me.

This Sunday Lula was wearing an old white dress that Marlene had given her. Only the night before they had worked on it like two schoolgirls, letting out and resewing the seams. Marlene felt the dress was too tight a fit, but since Lula wanted a new dress so badly, and since, even though it was tight, it was not quite vulgar, she lied to Lula and said that she felt Lula looked nice in it.

Father Jennings managed an occasional lustful glance in Lula's direction, but was more impressed by the way he had seen his superior staring at her. No, the old man was not quite lusting after her, but Father Jennings was certain that the rector had shown enough interest in Lula's voluptuous young body to indicate that he might easily be turned in that direction if Lula were to make herself available to him.

That night, after Marlene was asleep and Father Jennings and Lula had made love, or rather, after Lula had made love to him and he had taken from her, he told her of his plans to gain control of the church and what part she must play in those plans.

"That *old man,*" she said disgustedly.

"Yes," he said firmly, "that old man." He ran his fingers over her face tenderly and whispered, "And after that you'll live with me forever."

It was not difficult for Lula to get the old man alone,

but he was a strongly religious man, capable of resisting women who were even more experienced in ways of seduction than Lula. But in the end her youthful body and determination won and they became occasional bed partners. And finally, so desirous of her was he that he began to take her every week in the basement of the church in the sexton's bedroom. He would send the sexton off on an errand, allowing him the use of his car, knowing that the sexton would take the opportunity to enjoy the car for his own personal needs. At first the sexton was afraid that Father Walker would be angry with him for staying away from his duties for such long periods of time, but noticing that the rector never reprimanded him, he believed that the use of the car was the rector's way of rewarding him for cleaning the church so well, and he actually began to take more pride in his work.

Lula did not like using the sexton's bed, saying it smelled like the old man himself, and she had tried often to get the rector to make love to her elsewhere, but Father Walker was too old to assume the positions his younger assistant had been able to master and too religious to desecrate the actual body of the church. He felt it was bad enough that he used the basement as a place to fulfill his lust, but at least he had kept that lust confined to the basement and never allowed it to overflow in the presence of the sacrament.

During the months it had taken Lula to establish complete dominance over Father Walker, Jerome had been left alone a great deal, and he had established his own pattern of life. She had left him in the playground, thinking that he would remain there playing with the other children, but he had become a roamer, traveling to stores, restaurants, poolrooms, even other churches, where he talked with adults and where they, in turn, listened, enjoying the conversation of such a wise little boy.

Before long, that summer, the time of his fourth year, the entire neighborhood knew about Jerome. They called him the young evangelist. They called him Little Jesus. They called him the Black Knight of Christ. They called him a true son of God. When he entered any of the barbecue shops in the neighborhood, the owners or workers never failed to offer him all he could eat. And even if they had not been so kind to him, he still would have said words over the establishments in much the same way the old witch always said words over friendly houses. In the poolroom, he was allowed to sit in the owner's chair behind the cash register. It became such an impressive ceremony that all games stopped when he opened the door. "Watch that language, man, the little preacher's here," might be said by one of the players. As he passed the tables, they all watched and waited for him to climb the high stool. Once he had settled himself, he nodded and they continued to play.

The proprietor had commented jokingly that Jerome had turned his poolroom into a church. And he validated this by reminding people that since the "Black Knight of Christ" began visiting them there had not been one incident of violence. This in a place that had formerly averaged at least one incident a day for as long as the owner had been in business.

The same was true everywhere he went, for he was spreading the word of his God, sometimes just by his presence. But there was one exception to his behavior, and that, strange even to Jerome, was the emptiness of feeling that came over him when he was in the Episcopal church and every other church he had visited. At mass on Sunday, he now found himself unable to remain in his seat, excusing himself and wandering around out front watching the sun reflect from the many stained-glass windows, wondering in his young, troubled mind why he sensed so much evil in his Father's house.

And the evil was mounting. The old rector had changed so radically that those who had not seen him for a year or more found it difficult to believe that at his age he was actually beginning to look younger than he had ten years before. He walked faster now, smiling more often, and had suddenly found time to play with the children in the church playground, a thing he had not done in years. The parishioners noticed the change and it was whispered among them that he was undoubtedly having an affair with someone. "And at his age, too," one woman said teasingly to another.

"Well," the other woman replied, "if it's doing him that much good, God bless him."

His wife, too, noticed the change in him. And although she sensed it was being caused by another woman, she was thankful for it and would gladly have said so to the woman had she ever been confronted by her. She knew that on those nights that she was experiencing with increasing frequency of late when he turned to her and made love to her in ways he had never done before, he was thinking of someone else, but it did not matter because he had made her feel like a woman again.

It was true that he was not thinking of his wife. On those nights, after an afternoon with Lula had lingered in his mind for a day or two, the passion would flash through his body with such intensity that he would close his eyes, pretend his wife was the young girl, and treat her accordingly. Her flesh was much older than the young girl's, though, and often she went about her daily tasks in pain, but, remembering how each discomfort was caused, she would smile and relive the experience of the night or nights before.

Father Jennings had hoped that the rector's relationship with Lula would be discovered in a natural way. Lula had complained that she was tired of him, that he smelled of death, and that instead of getting weaker, he was becoming stronger every day, and now had begun to act like an animal.

Father Jennings told her she must hold out until they were discovered. "Listen," he said. "There's no way possible for him to go on the way he is without being caught sooner or later."

Her reply was simple and convincing. "Who caught *us?*"

The following Monday Father Jennings gave a small dinner party for the senior warden, two other vestrymen and their wives. The senior warden was usually the first to leave these events, and Lula arranged things so that she would be upstairs when he went to the washroom. She met him as he came out. "You've got to help me," she sobbed. "I've prayed for God to send someone to help me and it must be you."

He was completely befuddled. "There, there, child," he said gently. "The Lord finds help for all of us sooner or later."

"But I'm so ashamed I can't even tell you. Oh, Lord, forgive me. I don't do it because I want to. He makes me do it. He's made me do it for months and months and months now." She dried her eyes with her palms and he handed her his handkerchief.

"Now, now," he said in a fatherly way. "You just take your time and go ahead and tell me who you're talking about." He put his arm around her to comfort her and did not notice the eagerness with which she leaned against him. "Now you know I'm going to help you, so take your time and go ahead."

"At first," she said, now speaking very rapidly, "it was only maybe once a month, maybe not even that much, but then it got worse. Now it's every week, and sometimes two and three times a week. And I'm afraid, Mr. Jackson. I'm a good girl now. I don't do things like that anymore. And he won't use anything. And I told him I don't want to but he makes me do it. And I'm a good girl now. And suppose I get pregnant." She began crying again, and this time she mentioned the rector's name, saying that she loved the old man because everyone should love the rector and that she'd do anything he asked her to do because he was a man of God, but that this way of life seemed sinful to her.

And when she told the senior warden that she had spoken to the rector, saying that she thought it was wrong, and that the rector had told her that things she did with him were not sinful, that it was God's will that she satisfy him as he wished, the senior warden was so overcome with anger that he rushed downstairs and returned with Father Jennings so that the young curate could also stand as a witness against this sinful man.

The senior warden had given Lula the telephone number of his office, informing her that as soon as the old rector contacted her to make the appointment, she was to call him. Then he and Father Jennings would rush there and catch him before he was able to force her to have sex with him again. She had pretended to be frightened, afraid that they would not get there in time, but he assured her that if he was never able to do anything else in his life, he would see to it that she was not violated again.

Lula realized it would be a blessing to have such a religious man as the senior warden dedicated to her. If he were able to keep his promise, he would think of himself as her savior and glory in his righteous indignation; however, if he should arrive too late and find that she had indeed been "violated," his shame would make him her guilty servant. So when she called him, she gave the time of the meeting as fifteen minutes later than the time she and the rector had agreed upon.

After receiving the call, Mr. Jackson left his office so quickly that he did not have time to cancel his appointments for the rest of the day, stopped off to pick up Father Jennings, and the two men rushed to the church to save Lula. On the way there, Mr. Jackson told Father Jennings that the vestry had held a secret meeting and had voted to ask the rector to accept the elevation of Father Jennings from curate to co-rector. The meeting had been held several weeks ago and they were waiting until next month, the old man's thirtieth anniversary in the priesthood, to gift him with this surprise. It meant that they would also employ, finally, another priest, and the old rector would be able to remain on long after retirement age with this arrangement because his work load would have been considerably decreased. However, now that he had discovered that the rector had been living such a sinful life, all such plans would have to be abandoned. The rector would now be asked to resign.

"Do you think you can run things by yourself for a

while until we can find a suitable assistant for you, Father?"

"I'll do my best," Father Jennings replied humbly. "And with God's help, my best might be enough."

"I'm sure it will be. We're all very fond of you and your wife."

"Thank you, Mr. Jackson."

"No. Thank you. Your belief has been . . . well, your belief and your faith have been so strong that you've made even some of us crabby old ones reevaluate our lives and begin to think more in Christian terms. You've made this church more than a church. You've made it into a true Christian community."

At the church, they entered into the basement through the back door, and although they hurried they walked as softly as they could.

When they arrived at the door of the sexton's bedroom, the sounds they heard emanating from inside took them by such surprise that they exchanged quick glances of bewilderment and anger and, almost afraid of what they would find inside, they flung open the door and turned on the lights.

The rector was just reaching his climax, and so possessed was he by his passion that he did not care about the lights or whoever was standing behind him. He could not stop. And although Lula screamed and pretended to protest, with her fists flailing against his chest, her hips, moving ever so slightly, held him to her young body.

The senior warden and Father Jennings shouted at him, but he would not stop. He could not stop. Lula's contractions were coming so rapidly now that he could do nothing but follow her to that extended world of ecstasy she had taken him to so often. He had to finish if he was to be fulfilled.

Lula thought: Go on, you old sonofabitch. Enjoy yourself, 'cause it's the last time you will. She looked at the faces of the two men watching and thought how enjoyable it was to be *watched.* She beat the rector harder, striking him in the face as well as the chest now, knowing that each blow only excited him more; and all the while she was pulling, contracting, taking him deeper, repeatedly deeper and still deeper into her body, until she finally screamed and went into a wild hysterical frenzy, not of agony, but of absolute delight at what this day had brought to her.

Finally, the senior warden's rage mounted so that he grabbed the old man, flung him against the wall and began beating him.

Lula screamed, "Kill him! Kill him! Kill him!"

The rector fell to the floor and the senior warden began kicking him wildly, sinking his toe into his abdomen once, sending his heel glancing off his head another time.

Father Jennings had planned to let the beating go on for a while and then stop it, but now he was held captive by the senior warden's silent viciousness. And all the while Lula screamed, "Kill him! Kill him! Kill him! Kill him! Kill him!" But when he saw the blood pumping from the rector's face, he collected himself and went to his superior's aid. He restrained the senior warden, shouting, "For God's sake, Mr. Jackson, don't compound his sin by one of your own."

Lula's eyes were afire, and as she continued panting

heavily, she lowered her voice and whispered, "Kill the dirty old bastard. Kill him. Kill him."

After the senior warden had relaxed some, he was released. When his anger had subsided enough for him to focus on other things in the room, he found himself facing Lula, who was now sobbing uncontrollably. He picked up her clothing and handed it to her, all the while whispering, "Forgive me, child. I was certain we could get here in time to prevent this. Please. You've got to forgive me. Please forgive me. God, help her forgive me. I tried to get here on time. I tried to. God knows I . . ."

Lula did not respond, but merely left them to go to the ladies' room, where she dressed very slowly, smiling all the while.

"Get out of our church, you dirty old sonofabitch," the senior warden said with controlled anger as he threw the rector his clothing.

The rector, too, said nothing, he merely dressed and left, but the look in his eyes when he held his stare for an instant on Father Jennings made it evident to the young priest that the old man knew the scene just enacted had been planned from the very beginning.

On the way home, the senior warden promised Lula that if she helped them suppress what had happened to her so that the church was not disgraced, she would indeed, by contract from the vestry, be given a lifetime position somewhere in the church.

Lula said she would talk to him at another time, but not now. She was sick, she said, and felt like she was going to vomit.

He was understanding. "The strain's been too much

for you," he said. Then, turning to Father Jennings, he ordered, "Put this girl to bed for a few days. I'll see to it that a doctor and a nurse are sent to take care of her."

"Of course, Mr. Jackson. But the nurse won't be necessary. My wife and I can take care of her. Besides, she's done so much for us, we owe it to her."

The old rector was never heard from again. It was said that he went home, packed one bag and drove away. The parishioners now remembered that he had had a kind of faraway look in his eyes. Some even said they thought he had been insane all the while. And because only a very few of the vestrymen knew of his relationship with Lula, it was generally believed by most of the parishioners that since he had left his wife and deserted his parish, too, it must indeed have been because he had run off with that woman with whom he had been having that terrible affair for so many months. "Thank God for that young Father Jennings being around here or he might of stolen the church blind," they whispered among themselves.

Because there was some sympathy for the wife of the old rector, she was given a temporary pension of two thousand dollars for one year. After that time she would have to arrange some way to care for herself. But she was asked to move out of the big house so that the new rector could have it.

Within a month Father Jennings, his wife, Lula and Jerome moved into the big house, only now Marlene and Lula divided the household duties equally. Marlene did not mind sharing her house with Lula. If anything, she was happy to be able to treat Lula as her equal because without Lula's silence the disgrace that would come to the parish could be so overwhelming that it might ruin her husband's career, too. A house run by two women would normally have been an impossible house, but Marlene was a master of compromise. Whenever Lula pushed unreasonably for her way, Marlene acquiesced, feeling that that was the only Christian thing to do.

Several months later the rector's automobile was found abandoned in San Diego, but still there was no mention of him.

The day Lula discovered she was pregnant again she was thrown into a continuous state of depression. This was not at all the way she had called on the demons to render her with child. If she had this child, it would be the same as before. Father Jennings would say it was not his. And this time there would be even less doubt in his mind than there had been with Jerome. He would say it was the child of the old man. He would say he was through with her. He would say he would have nothing else to do with her. She knew she could force him to treat her the way she wanted, and that in the end she would still own him. The devils had promised her this. They would not renege on their promise. But how could she possibly continue to keep the old ladies of the church on her side? She could not now say that her condition was the result of being raped by the rector. That was impossible at this time. In protecting the parish from the scandal, in allowing herself to be used by them, she had indeed put herself in a most vulnerable position.

She had wanted it to be Father Jennings' child so unquestionably that he would feel compelled to defend her and ultimately leave the wife who could never give him children. He would divorce Marlene and marry her and they would go away to another church and he could still practice his ministry. But he would never divorce Marlene now—not for this bastard child. She hated Marlene. She had always hated her, but now she hated her more than she believed she was ever capable of hating anyone.

Once she had thought of a plan to get Marlene to leave. It had been such a simple thing that one would think it could not possibly fail, but it did. Father Jennings had come to her bedroom that night as he so often did, and when they were making love she pretended to be so thrilled by him that she could not help crying out. Her outcry had awakened Marlene and Marlene had come out of her bedroom to determine the cause of the disturbance, but it had taken Marlene so long to find her robe and button it completely before she stepped into the hallway that Father Jennings, sensing his discovery was imminent, hurriedly slipped into his robe, rushed out of Lula's room and, when discovered by his wife, appeared to be closing the door of Jerome's bedroom.

"What was that?" Marlene asked.

"Jerome was having a nightmare," he said calmly. "He's all right now. He won't remember it, though, because I don't think he even woke up."

"I was so frightened when I woke up and didn't find you next to me. I couldn't imagine what had happened. It sounded like a woman's scream and my first thought was that someone had broken in, perhaps had even killed you, and was then attacking Lula."

He put his arm around her and they walked back to their bedroom. He noticed that she was trembling and he felt quite warm and manly next to her. "It's all right, darling," he said. "Nothing like that could ever happen to us." Her fragility made him feel ever so secure in his manhood.

"I don't know what I would have done if anything had happened to you," she said as they lay down in bed. Then she sat up with a start. "Oh, my God—Lula! What if something really terrible has happened to her and we don't even know it?"

"Everything's fine. I looked in on her," he said casually, "and she didn't even wake up."

"Then I guess she sleeps even more soundly than I do," Marlene said.

Father Jennings turned on his side and sighed, "Yes, I guess she does."

Lula was angry that that plan had not worked, and since it had not, she prayed to the monsters of her night that she might have another child by Father Jennings. They had never been wrong before. Why would they let her down now? she wondered as she sat there in church watching Father Jennings celebrate his first mass as rector of the church. Why would they begin to lie to her now?

The night before, she had sat in a tub of water so hot that it almost scalded her. She had taken heavy laxatives and quinine and, finally, sat on the toilet probing what she hoped was the entrance to her uterus with a hairpin until the pain was so great that she could stand it no longer.

All of these things had failed, and although she was feeling a great deal of discomfort from her efforts to induce an abortion, she had resigned herself to the acceptance of another bastard child.

She looked at Jerome and thought: Why can't you be old enough so that I can ask you directly to help me? Why the hell aren't you old enough so you can do some witchcraft or something? And at this moment Father Jennings turned to face the congregation and chanted, "Let us go forth in peace, Alleluia."

And the congregation responded, "In the name of Christ, Amen."

The service had ended and the recessional had begun.

While this was happening, Lula's mind was evoking Jerome's name, and the little boy looked at his mother forgivingly.

It was at this moment when she looked at him, seeing his deep eyes penetrating her soul, that she felt the first really severe pains, and the blood running down the inner side of her legs, and then she fainted. But she could not forget, taking into her unconscious state the memory of Jerome's eyes, all knowing, looking at her in a way that, for some reason unanswerable to her, made her feel shame.

They rushed her to the hospital, where she remained for two weeks. This stay in the hospital was nothing like her last one. Before, she had been in a maternity ward that was so overcrowded she occupied one of the many beds that had been set up in the hallway. She was only a charity patient and it seemed to her that every intern and resident in the hospital looked at her sutures and examined her abdomen. The nurses and nurses' aids were crass and often inconsiderate of her, forcing her to make her own bed and walk the full length of the enormous ward to pick up her food tray. Once finished, she was told she must return it herself. And still there was further degradation, for shortly before she was permitted to check out of the hospital she was put to work by a nurses' aid cleaning the toilet.

Now, however, it was all different. The vestry of Saint Luke's Episcopal Church saw to it that she was placed in a private room and received the best of nursing care. Her physician was one of the vestrymen who knew of the scandal, and her case was diagnosed as a "spontaneous abortion." It was an enjoyable two-week experience.

During Lula's period of hospitalization, Marlene and Jerome spent much time in each other's company. Jerome found it difficult to be alone because Marlene was so protective of him. Once he disappeared for five hours and Marlene was frightened that some tragedy had befallen him. When he returned home, she told him he must be punished, but before doing that, she wanted him to tell her where he had been for so many hours.

"I've been visiting with my people, doing my Father's work," he replied calmly.

He had always amazed her, this little child who was so grown-up. And now, loving him as much as she did, she was forced to smile and forget the punishment. "You must be starved," she said. "Let's you and me sit down and have lunch."

"I'm not hungry, thank you. My people fed me."

"Well, surely you'll have a glass of milk with me?"

Jerome nodded.

After they were seated in the kitchen for a while, Marlene finally found a way to broach the question. "Jerome," she said, almost fearing what his reply might be, "just who are your people?"

"They are my Father's people," he said. "The same as you are."

"Can *I* meet your people?"

The little boy's face flashed with joy. "Oh, yes. Can we go tomorrow? I promised them I would be back tomorrow. They've missed me." He got down from his seat and put his arms around her neck and she felt a strange comfort, one so warming that it confused her. "I would like you to go with me. Will you take me tomorrow, please?"

"Yes, yes," she answered happily. "We'll go first thing in the morning."

"We can't go until afternoon," Jerome answered. "But we can spend the morning with the old lady who is so good."

Marlene awakened and was surprised to find Jerome sitting in the chair near her bed, smiling at her.

"Good morning," he said.

She rubbed the sleep from her eyes, looked at the clock and saw that it was only five o'clock. "Jerome," she said in a whisper so as not to awaken Father Jennings. "It's too early. Go back to sleep. I'll call you when it's time to get up."

"You didn't forget about today?" he asked eagerly.

She smiled. "No, I did not forget."

After he left, Marlene fell into a deep sleep and

dreamed she was walking in darkness through a quaint city. It was warm in her dream and she thought the warmth and heavy vegetation meant she was in the tropics. She remembered being amazed that although it was so black of night, she was experiencing no fear as she walked along the city streets. People smiled and greeted her in a most friendly manner. She had been walking for a long time, but she was not yet tired. There were many beautifully styled thatched-roof houses, and oil lanterns flickered their uneven light out the windows, lighting her way to a fountain at that part of town which turned out to be the town square. When she reached the square, she took a seat on the ground along with the hundreds of other people who had gathered to listen to a man talk. It was so dark now that she could not see the faces or style of dress of anyone, but still she was not afraid. Indeed, she felt comfortable in the darkness—not at all as she was in real life, where night frightened her because she thought of it as a time of evil. But the night of her dream was different. The blackness of the sky, the ground, the people about her—the only light now being that from the horizon, which made all the figures seen against it seem like only a lighter black—was a warming blackness that seeped into her body and gave off a spirit of its own that thrilled and warmed her at the same time.

She strained to hear the man, but his words seemed to pass by her. Then, as if the winds were bringing them back to her ears alone, they echoed for her, and she was able to hear fragments of his message. ". . . This is only one of many lives for all of you. . . . I therefore say that you must make the most of this life. . . . It will be a long time before you go through and join me. . . . No, there is no hell. . . . Heaven? Here. . . . No, I am the last one to come. . . . In a few hundred years I will come again, but you will be different people by then. . . . No, there is no hell. . . . Heaven?" Marlene could hear the smile in his voice. She got to her feet to ask him what he meant by the things she had heard him say. As she neared him, he turned and walked away. She called to him and without turning around he said, "Be at peace, Marlene, for the next life will be better."

Later that morning at breakfast, Marlene told Father Jennings of her dream and he teased her, saying that he knew all along that she was not a Christian.

"This proves beyond a doubt that you believe in reincarnation."

They laughed.

After breakfast, Father Jennings carried Jerome to the door with him. "And what do you think of dreams, young man?"

"I believe what my Father has told me. I believe in everlasting life."

"Aha," he teased. "There. You see. Straight from the young prophet. A life hereafter, but no reincarnation." He kissed Marlene and Jerome, and left.

In walking through his back yard and across the alley to the church, he thought of Jerome and said to himself: I wish the hell I could get him to stop saying "My Father." He did not know why, but lately Jerome had begun to make him uncomfortable. He thought about the deep, piercing black eyes of Jerome and a chill went through his body. How the hell can a child that young have such an old face? he asked himself. He's not normal. I never heard of a five-year-old who could sit around the house for a full day and be so quiet. Something's wrong here. Sometimes it's almost as if he's just recording things, storing them in that wise little head of his. He paused to pick up a piece of brown paper that was trapped in one of the rosebushes, and when he straightened up there was a new thought suddenly exploding within his mind. What if he's not really as smart as we all seem to think he is? What if he's really retarded! No, no child of mine could be retarded. Then he realized that he had finally acknowledged Jerome as his son. This, too, terrified him, and he seemed to be more convinced than ever that Jerome was not at all the exceptional child they had all thought him to be, but rather an idiot who had picked up (through being in his presence, of course) a few phrases that he had discovered produced a favorable reaction in people and used them repeatedly to win praise. He had studied enough psychology, he thought, to know that the insane ones were the ones who sometimes appeared to be geniuses.

When he was settled at his desk, he made an appointment with a psychological testing laboratory for the following month. By now he was thoroughly convinced that Jerome was insane and should perhaps be put in a home for the mentally ill. Besides, he thought, he's beginning to give me the creeps. He's got to be sick. There's no way in the world a child his age can be that quiet and still be normal.

When Marlene and Jerome reached the attic dwelling of the old lady, Jerome opened the door and started in.

"Jerome," Marlene said angrily, "you shouldn't just walk into someone's home unannounced."

"It's all right," he said. "She knows we're coming. She always knows when I'm coming."

Then, from inside, the voice of the old woman called out, "Come in, Jerome, and bring your friend with you."

Once the door was shut behind them, Marlene realized that she had encountered the very same darkness of her dream and the same warmth and the same comfort. Before her eyes could adjust, Jerome was leading her toward the light coming through the small window at the other end of the apartment. There were no partitions, only one long room with one window.

"Watch your head," the old woman said.

Then Marlene realized that the steeply pitched roof limited one's movements even more. She found it to be very warm, but not uncomfortable, and her senses were excited by the smell of the room. From what she could discern, there were many aromas mingling to produce what she thought surely must be the same smell one would encounter in a greenhouse filled with exquisite flowers.

As they neared the window, she saw the old woman kneel at Jerome's feet, then take a seat on a stool. At first she thought the woman's actions amusing, but then she realized that this was not merely a game played by an old woman with a five-year-old; there was an air of reverence about her.

Jerome took a seat in a high-backed wicker chair, stained from age, and motioned for Marlene to seat herself in a chair nearer the old woman. She kept thinking the scene she was seeing must be a comedy, but some strange force willed that she respond to Jerome's wishes and remain silent.

"I've brought Marlene to you that together you might continue the work of my Father," Marlene heard the little boy say. Then he turned to her and said, "This is Thelma. She is a witch."

Marlene looked quickly at the old woman.

Sensing Marlene's fear, the witch spoke quickly. "The Father has ordained that some of us must go about His work in ways strange to most people."

And for some reason unknown to Marlene, she found herself nodding in understanding, with absolutely no fear. She sat back and looked around the room searchingly as Jerome and the old woman spoke softly but cryptically, so strangely that she could not understand them. She noticed a bed, one chest, two tables, one very low, which held a hot plate, the stool on which the witch was now seated and the two chairs she and Jerome occupied. Then the woman was before her offering a cup of something.

"It is tea," she said comfortingly. "Only tea."

Marlene nodded her thanks and took the cup, realizing that the tea had been made while she had been examining the room. She also realized that the water had been boiling when they came in, and that there was incense burning somewhere in the room, even though she could not see the smoke. Perhaps it was only a perfume of some kind, she told herself. She smiled to herself, wondering how it was that a dark attic could be so comfortable. She drank her tea and had more before she realized that Jerome, too, was drinking tea. Then she wondered what strange thing it was that had happened to her. Why was she so slow to notice things? Why was she unable to speak? And why, why had she suddenly felt the urge to kiss Jerome's hand, or just to touch him?

Then Marlene felt her mind cloud, as if a soft shutter in it had closed, dulling it, filtering out certain things. She felt that she must have been drugged. The tea. The tea, she thought. And then, as if she were again experiencing a dream, she heard Jerome say, "I shall return once again and then no more."

The old woman nodded and said, "Yes, Lord."

"Strange how much more difficult it is this time. We are all so different in this life."

Then the shutter in her mind seemed to dissolve slowly and she realized that it had not been a dream. Suddenly she was so overcome with happiness that she began crying.

Jerome turned to her and smiled. Then he said, "Come, Marlene, we must visit the others."

How could it be? she asked herself as she followed the child Jerome out the door. How could it be?

The next few hours were equally amazing to Marlene.

She was terrified when Jerome took her to the first tavern, and the house of the prostitutes, where the women gathered around him and sat on the floor while he told of the nobility of their profession. At first the women were made uncomfortable by Marlene's presence, but Jerome put them at ease, saying, "Marlene is one of the few people of God I have met within the church." In this house she was given coffee, only now there was no dulling influence at work within her mind. Now she could see Jerome's saintly nature clearly and she was not frightened of him. She only wanted to serve him, to serve him in any way possible. She realized that he had done something to her so that her mind would be able to adjust gradually to the knowledge he had given her. She was thankful that he had brought her along gradually so that the shock of such a discovery would not be extreme.

They left the house of the prostitutes, stopping at restaurants, poolrooms, more taverns and finally one last barbecue shack, where they were fed by the proprietor. And everywhere his followers spoke to him softly, with reverence. In all, she could not remember exactly how many places they had visited, but she thought it to be at least ten or twelve, and she did remember that in each place there had been at least one person who appeared to be closest to him.

They walked home in silence, for Marlene realized he wanted it thus. As they entered the back door, they heard Father Jennings coming in the front way.

"They must not know," Jerome said.

"I understand."

"Everything must appear as it was."

"Yes, Lord," she said glowingly.

Jerome smiled and ascended the stairs at the rear of the house to his bedroom, where he remained for the rest of the day. Later that evening Marlene took dinner to him, telling Father Jennings that he was running a temperature and should be kept in bed for a while.

Father Jennings did not question her further about Jerome, nor did he go to visit with him at any time during the next week when the child was absent from his presence. He was relieved not to have him around, and he began to assume a more relaxed attitude, telling himself how wonderful it would be when the child was finally put away.

Father Jennings brought Lula home from the hospital. Jerome saw her come through the doorway and ran to her. The instant he put his arms around her neck she saw the monsters at their work on the walls and ceiling; there were even some on the floor, growing like vegetation from the spot where Jerome had stood. She took his hands from around her neck and put him back on the floor, where, to her surprise, he walked unmolested among the monsters. A shiver went through her and she thought, stay with your own kind, dammit. And at this the monsters performed so furiously that she was confused. In the past they had danced in this manner only when she had pleased them. Surely the thought she had just had about Jerome could not be considered complimentary by them. But perhaps it could. Perhaps everything about them was different. Perhaps she was even wrong to have been so good to Jerome, or even to have claimed him as her child. After all, he did belong to them. She was only his mother. And even this she was now beginning to question. They could have made a mistake at the hospital—or one of the devils could have put himself into Jerome's body, or they could have gotten a nurse to put this beast she called her son, she thought, in the place of her real son. But if none of this was true, if Jerome really was her son, who in God's name *was* his father?

Lula started to her room, being careful to keep as much distance as possible between herself and Jerome, relieved, finally, that the creatures had left her at peace for a while. As she started up the stairs she called back to Jerome. "Why don't you go out and play for a while?" she said.

"I'll take him," Marlene said.

"Oh. Hello, Marlene," said Lula, noticing her for the first time. "Would you, please? I'm still not able to get around too well yet."

"Don't even think about it. We go out every day at about this time."

Later that evening Father Jennings told Lula that the vestry had decided that she should enroll in secretarial school as a full-time student. Marlene would stay home to care for Jerome.

Marlene was not present when this marvelous news

was told to Lula, but when she and Jerome returned, Father Jennings told her that it was the desire of the vestry that Lula do this so that she might assume the position of secretary for the church.

Marlene agreed to his wishes, but asked, "What about the secretary you already have? She's been here for twenty years and this is her only means of support."

Father Jennings shouted angrily, "It's up to the vestry to determine what they want to do with her. I can't think for everybody all the time. You act like you don't want Lula to have the job."

"Oh, no. Of course I want her to have it." And there was no further discussion.

As Marlene was preparing the evening meal, she thought about the way her husband had raised his voice at her. Lately this seemed to be the only way he could speak to her, and she wondered how long it would be before he began to beat her.

He had changed so much since . . . since . . . When did he start changing? she asked herself. He was not at all like his old self now that he was rector. Now that things were going exactly as he wanted, he seemed more unhappy with her than ever. He seemed to her as if he was irritated with her presence, and if he wasn't shouting at her, he was talking to her through a magazine or a Bible or behind his back. That he never looked at her anymore unless they were in public, as if he were nurturing a great shame, hurt her more than the shouting.

Their lives had altered considerably, too. Now they were frequent guests of other priests throughout the diocese, and also of the bishop. The bishop had even honored them by saying a special mass in their home. So many good and exciting things had happened to them, and yet Father Jennings seemed to withdraw into himself a little more with each new wonderful thing that came their way.

It had been rumored that he was to be made dean over all other rectors in his area of the city, most of them being considerably older than he, and it had also been said that this was only a means of getting him in a position of higher respect to make him more readily acceptable to the church hierarchy so that the bishop would have no objectors when he appointed Father Jennings to his advisory board. And it was whispered that this move, too, was only a beginning, that the young priests in the diocese wanted new, younger bishops, and they were willing to back Father Jennings, if not for this diocese, then perhaps for another one. It was almost certain that he would become a bishop in ten or fifteen years, and he would be the youngest bishop in modern times ever elected by the Council of Bishops. If his friends were smart and careful enough, they could move him from one influential position to another so that when his name was put on the ballot, he would win easily over the opposition.

Marlene felt certain that Father Jennings would become a bishop, but she was troubled about their relationship. It was almost as if each positive thing that happened to him in his profession had an equally negative effect on their marriage. It was true that they still slept in the same bed, but now they were like strangers who crawled into bed completely clothed and lay as far from each other as possible.

While Lula was in the hospital he was out almost every night and sometimes she would awaken in the morning and find that he had not come home at all. Once she questioned him about this and he said that he had had so much to drink at the bishop's house that the bishop would not let him drive home, and made him stay there to sleep it off. Another time he had come in smelling so heavily of perfume that, again, she was moved to question him about the evening, but only after she had gotten up the courage to do so three days later.

He told her that a friend of the bishop had come to town with his wife, and that his wife had gotten drunk and sprinkled perfume over everybody at the little gathering. He would have taken her to the party, he said, but he did not think she would have been able to get a sitter for Jerome, so he went alone, not wanting to make her feel bad about having to miss it. "Actually," he said, "it wasn't a very good party, anyway. Besides, I don't like your being around all those drunks. It's not the kind of thing a woman like you should see."

Once she needed and wanted him so badly that she tried to seduce him. Her feelings were irreparably shattered when he rejected her, saying that she had shocked and disappointed him by her conduct, that he could not understand what had come over her that made her suddenly act like a woman of the street. Then he lectured her further, saying that he was troubled about their sex life, because sex was not only for enjoyment, and perhaps their not wanting to have a child was comparable to living in sin. He wasn't sure and he was going to take the matter up with the bishop. And if his thoughts were confirmed, he might have to become a celibate like the bishop.

Marlene was so humiliated that she cried herself to sleep that night on the couch in the living room, and swore never to approach him again. If he wanted to live the life of a celibate, he could. She would not stand in his way. She herself would make no promises to him, to God or to anyone else, but she would never offer herself to him again. At first she was tormented by her desire for him. Now that it seemed he would have sex with her no more, her drive was so strong that she thought about almost nothing else during the day. How could it be fair to expect her to give up a God-given privilege when she was so young, when it was all new to her, and when she was just beginning to be free enough to move from the extremely passive person she had been to one who was finally willing to participate equally with her partner? Years before she had been resentful when he asked her to perform certain acts, feeling they were abnormal. Since she was his wife, however, she felt she must obey him and do what he wanted, and she did, but she did so resentfully. Now, however, she had become a woman, no longer the frightened little girl so terrified of every new experience, and she was willing not only to follow, but to lead him in experimenting in the art of love. Life had become so cruel to her, she had thought, for now that she was at last mature, he had closed off this part of her life, almost as if he had chosen this method to punish her for not understanding when she was younger.

But none of this mattered now, for Marlene had found comfort in her God in Heaven and her God on earth. Jerome had ordained that she was to work for Him and she no longer had the need for self. She had been touched by God; therefore she had been given the gift of ultimate satisfaction.

The day before Jerome was to be taken to the testing laboratory, he set fire to the church. The sexton was off duty. Marlene was away at a guild meeting only a few blocks from there and Father Jennings and Lula were upstairs in Lula's room.

When Father Jennings looked out the window and saw the smoke, he was thrown into a state of shock because he also saw Jerome leaving the basement of the church.

"That little monster," he shouted as he pulled on a pair of pants and hurried out of the room.

Lula was close behind him, screaming, "He's evil. He's a monster. He's the devil himself."

As they turned into the kitchen, they encountered Jerome. He had just taken a knife out of the drawer and placed it on the table against the wall.

Father Jennings grabbed his arm and flung him away from the table and began slapping him. "Why did you do this, you little monster?"

Jerome did not cry out. He merely picked himself up

each time he was struck and waited to be struck again. And when asked why he had set fire to the church, he replied in a tone that they had never heard him use before, in the voice of an old man. "Because it is not the house of *my* Father."

"*Your* father," the priest shouted. "You little bastard. You have no father." He struck Jerome several times again with the belt he had pulled from his trousers, not caring that the leather was cutting into the flesh of his face and head and back.

All this time Lula was screaming insults at the little boy and slapping at him when his small body passed near her. Then she saw the monsters again, only now they were laughing, hundreds, thousands of them, deformed animal people laughing so loud that she cried out from the pain the noise caused to her head.

Father Jennings was caught up so completely with the insanity of the moment, sobbing, shouting, perspiration sliding down his face from his hair and mingling with his tears, that he beat Jerome with all the fury of someone who was destroying a poisonous reptile that had almost bitten him. Then he stopped, let out a scream himself and stood there trembling in terror as he noticed Jerome bleeding from the palms of his hands.

Lula screamed, "He's the devil! I told you he was evil. Only a devil would pretend to be Jesus. Grab him! Grab him! Grab him!" And as Father Jennings held Jerome's arms, Lula took the knife from the table, the noise of the devils all about her, piercing her body so that she screamed even louder in her fanatical state, and leaped toward Jerome, sinking the knife into his young chest again, again, again . . . screaming all the while with Father Jennings, "The devil! The devil!"

When Marlene and other members of the parish burst in, Lula, standing in a pool of blood, was still stabbing him and Father Jennings, his eyes locked in a trance, was holding him off the floor by his arms, yelling, "Kill the devil! Kill the devil! Kill the devil!"

epilogue

That night, the night of Jerome's death, the owners of the neighborhood bars were irritable because it was the most unproductive Saturday night in recent history. The residents mourned the loss of the little boy as if he had been a saint, and a strange heaviness settled over the area. The streets were almost peopleless for the entire night. Those few who did go out of doors that night noticed no strange phenomena taking place to explain what they sensed, but, nevertheless, they experienced fear. There was the feeling of doom, the feeling of having lost their salvation. No one could explain the uneasiness that had settled upon their lives.

But if one had been on the street early in the morning when the old witch was returning to her attic dwelling, one would have seen her turn her head to the sky and scream, "They've killed the Black Jesus."

world of nothing

To be perfectly honest with you, I can't see anywhere to go. Even if I could, I'm not sure I'd want to leave my beautiful World of Nothing to get there. I mean, what assurance do I have once I arrive at my destination—whatever it is—that it's going to be any better than here. Nothing is a positive place where there is beauty and joy and love and friendship, and I'm not so sure I want to be removed from the state. My Nothing is real, alive; it swings to the tune of "Rock My Soul in the Bosom of Abraham."

Nothing is a state of black. It's a world where the only white face is an occasional policeman or the peddler or the store owners or those goddamn insurance men. But mostly it's all black. It's even black when the sun beats down on our shiny faces; the rays seem to soak into our world and shatter and form a black cloud that hangs like a gloomy continuation of night symbolic of the segregated quarters wherein we eat and laugh and love and cry and live and die. It's like the fixed wall of public housing down State Street in Chicago that the city mothas have graciously provided as living symbols of segregation to stand in their honor for the next hundred or so years.

red top evolves into our nothing

Red Top and I share a two-room apartment out here in Nothing. We've lived here for two years and will probably stay put until they raise the rent or until a highway comes through or some kind of urban renewal. It's a nice place if you like old obsolete buildings and substandard living. We used to have a cat here, but the rats chased him away about a year ago. We used to wash walls and windows and sweep the place once in a while, too, but it just gets that way again, so what's the use.

I remember how it looked when we moved in and how we put Black Flag down all around the rooms every night before we went to bed until the people in the other apartments complained that we were disturbing the equal distribution of roaches and threatened to kick us out if we didn't accept our share of the bastards and stop trying to be such aristocrats. We live in a democracy out here and we didn't want to make enemies of our neighbors, so we accepted our quota and learned to live with them.

Red Top is my roommate, and quite obviously he's a Negro. He has a real name but I've forgotten it. I guess he's what you'd call a handsome man; about eight inches over five feet, 175 pounds, a head full of nappy red hair, gray eyes that slant upward slightly and practically no beard at all. He manages to stay in pretty good shape for his age and he's quite popular. He never has to *buy* any—he says. Well, that's what he says, anyway. I should be half so lucky. My checks might go a lot farther if I didn't have to pass a little around among the ladies' lingerie lounges and at supermarkets for that occasional loaf of bread or bottle of wine. I get most if it back, though. In time I'll get it all back from them.

People like Red Top, and sometimes they come by to visit and bring little things for us. Sometimes women bring food, and, of course, he shares *that* with me.

Red Top gets out more than I do. Sometimes he stays out all day.

Once they locked him up for two weeks as a material witness in a murder trial. I thought he was dead. It seemed like a logical assumption to me. He didn't come home, so he must have been dead. I was a little disappointed when he finally returned because I had already cashed his check and spent most of it. He was disturbed about this. He's a pretty vicious guy sometimes. I had to get a job to pay him back—two *weeks* he made me work just for *money*. And then he made me pay the rent myself.

We understand each other, though, and the arrangement works pretty good most of the time.

Red Top is not a native of the city. Is anybody? He was born on a farm, the son of a sharecropper who was the son of a sharecropper who was the son of a slave—

the son of a white man's slave; the son of a son of a bitch. He got a chance to break away from home during the big war, when he was drafted into the army as a cook, and after he had helped free the rest of the world he came back home to become a modern-day slave in the great U.S. of A.

He fought the old ways for a while, joining every group that promised him equality and freedom, but always ended up being investigated by the Feds for membership in a subversive organization. Any damn organization with letters is communist inspired, and any movement to correct an existing deformity is communist inspired, and any outspoken critic of the "Good Old American Way" (whatever the hell that is) is stamped and sealed communistic. And Red Top was one of the hottest communistic noncommunists in the U.S.A.

They shook him up so he was afraid to sign his name on a pledge card in church. He was smart, aggressive and on the way up, good job and all, but he wanted to charge out in front of the ranks carrying the flag of the cause. And he did; when he looked around for the rest of the troops they were miles behind him and nobody was near to defend him when they pulled the flag away and cut him up in little pieces and left him for dead—and left him dead, spiritually without substance, without soul—*dead!*

He drifted around the country for a few years after that, sleeping where he could and living from time to time, but dying away a little more every day.

We bumped into each other one day outside the Cut-Rate Liquor Store. We were both standing outside waiting for one of the guys to come out with a bottle of wine and let us have a taste, when three little punks appeared with a basket of bottles they had collected throughout the neighborhood and brought to the store to cash in for the grand deposit. When the kids came out I took their basket and started to amass my own personal fortune. Red Top followed me down the alley. We struck up a conversation, joined forces and spent the afternoon searching for bottles and talking about Nothing and the effect it has on the rest of the city.

The kids had stripped the alleys clean—we could find only a half-dozen bottles; scarcely enough for a pint of wine and a loaf of bread. When we got back to the store there was a pop truck parked at the curb. The driver and his helper were inside restocking the place when we hit on the idea to take the empties right off the truck. "You get the bottles and I'll watch these cats," Red Top said.

I began unloading the truck. As I'd take a case off the truck, I'd hurry around to the side of the building and hide it among the boxes piled there. I got twenty cases of empties before Red Top alerted me. After the truck left, we carried the cases down the alley and stacked them where they'd be safe for a while and then returned to the store with enough bottles for *two* pints of wine. We turned in a few others at the grocery store and got bologna and bread. The idea to buy food came from Red Top. I wanted to drink it all up but he's the kind of guy who has to take care of his stomach since it's all fouled up. I sort of felt he had the right idea, but it was a strange feeling to spend money for food instead of begging for it. Buy what you want and beg for what you need—that's been my philosophy out here for years. It's always worked. Why should I suddenly have to buy food when it's out there if you stand long enough and put it on—I mean, really strong—for some good-natured chump?

We've got all kinds of do-gooders walking around just praying to find somebody begging for a meal. But they always have to give you a lecture, the bastards. They say it just before they drop the money in your hand (of course they drop it; you think they want to touch your hand?) and it always sounds the same way: "Now you're sure you won't use this to buy yourself a drink?" Or they say: "Now get something to eat." And you stand there smiling and lying and agreeing to anything they say so they'll let go of the change and drop it into your damn hand and you can take off and get some bread and cheese or bologna or a cup of coffee and most of all a pint of something that's *really* drinkable.

They don't give you that much, though; just nickels and dimes—just small change to help ease their conscience.

Once in a while they'll try to proposition you, too, like the cat who asked me to go to bed with his sister so he could watch us. She was a nut about Negroes—she was a nut about men—and he was another kind of nut who was nuts about her being nuts about Negroes. And then there was the old lady about nine hundred years old and the little fairy (he's always around; he's a safety valve for some of us), and all kinds of weird people.

So Red Top and I got along pretty good. We got on relief about the same time and moved into this crummy place and have been here ever since. At first I used to go out and find odd jobs, but that got to be too much and I decided to just stay home. Sometimes I write. Sometimes I read. Sometimes I write. Sometimes I read. I write a lot of stuff, but I don't get it published because I don't have the money to waste on stamps and all that jazz. Most of the time I get drunk—that's making sense out of life.

Red Top worked for a while but the welfare officer caught up with him and was taking fifty percent of his pay as a kickback and Red Top said to hell with him; why should the white man get rich off him? He quit the job and now just takes it easy like me and has a little hustle going at night down the street in one of the houses; he sort of sees to it that the girls are properly protected before, during and after. I think that's why he never has to buy it. He says it's not true but I know it is—he's not that good. Nobody is. Everybody has to pay. Sooner or later everybody has to pay.

It's a sort of a quiet life we lead here; no television or radio to distract us from our thoughts and dreams and drinks. For a long time we had a rather interesting schedule for the first week of the money—what with money being plentiful and dwindling away to absolutely nothing by the middle of the month. Beginning with Monday, we'd start out at Marovitz's grocery store to find out what had taken place over the weekend. Standing in front of the meat counter, we'd listen to the women relate their long narratives about Susan's kitchenette whippin', or Sam's encounter with the book who never pays on time, or Big P. bailing a couple of his girls out of jail.

"And, Mr. Marovitz, you shoulda seed her when she came runnin' out of her room. Why, she had blood all over her and not a stitch of clothes on—not even . . . well, just not a stitch."

Mr. Marovitz's eyes would light up and he would be lost to the story and not see the children stealing candy bars. For that matter, he wouldn't even see me and Red Top stealing.

"Well, I sure saw that woman," a lady interrupted. "She bust right into my place and begged me to help her. And all the time my husband, the damn fool, he just standin' there smilin' like some stupid ass—he just smilin' and lookin'. I gave her my housecoat and told her I didn't want no blood on it and I wanted it back."

We'd hang around there until we found out where they were holding the inquest. That's right, the inquest. Monday without an inquest would have been like Monday without daylight, it would have been like Monday without breathing. We had to have an inquest because somebody always got killed over the weekend, by either car or knife, or a policeman, or a gun or heroin or a policeman or falling from a window, or a policeman. . . . Anything but suicide. We don't do that. We leave suicide for white people because they're fragile and can't take it. Suicide is for the whites because they've got everything. Suicide is for the whites because they don't have anything.

So by Monday morning the weekend of drinking had caught up with us and it was a pleasure to sit in a quiet funeral parlor and smell the flowers and listen to the witnesses lie, everybody blaming the dead man or woman. The flowers were always pretty. We got to love this time of the week—the clean floors, the high ceilings, the beautiful flower arrangements, the various scents filling the room. We got so we enjoyed the damn places so much we started stopping by in the evenings during the middle of the week to see if there was a wake going on—the black Pat and Mike paying our respects to the bereaved family.

If we were lucky and didn't look too bad they might invite us by for a drink afterward. We had some swinging wakes; sometimes Red Top would make out with the cat's wife or aunt or cousin or maybe even his brother. I never made out with anyone, but then I never do, so that's not too important.

After leaving the inquest on this first day of the first week of the month, our checks in our pockets, we'd go back to Mr. Marovitz's store, cash the checks, bring the food accounts up to date, and head for the hottest spot on the street—Herb's Barbershop. Everybody was there. They loved the place. The guys in show business staying at the hotel used the shop as their conversation corner during the day. A few of the policy runners with their little books would stop in between deliveries on their runs and joke with the rest of the sitters, sitting around living and reliving the weekend before they cut out to start back to the hustle. Herb was about forty —he's always been about forty, except he's losing his hair now and can no longer stand in front of the mirror combing and pushing his pomp—and used to be a little on the heavy side before he started playing golf. Everybody started playing golf at about the same time because the money got big for all of them at about the same time and the courses began to open up (a couple of them, anyway) and take Negroes in on a large scale. Herb was happy, smooth and dapper; everyone loved him. He had a superb memory and could recall vividly incidents that happened when he first came to the city, at the age of nine. He knew everybody and didn't seem to be impressed with status one way or the other. Oh, he respected authority and was pleased when someone who grew up with him made the big time, but it didn't really move him. He just liked people and didn't give a damn where they came from or what line they were in so long as they conducted themselves like gentlemen when they were in his establishment.

Herb had a barber working with him back a few years ago—well, before that he had three barbers working there, but that was during the war, when things were really good—and the cat couldn't leave the bottle alone. Herb wouldn't let his barbers drink in the shop, so you'd see the cat cut awhile, talk awhile, cut awhile, and then step outside and around the corner to a place where he stashed his pint and then come sheepishly back to his customer, making some excuse about not being able to get his throat cleared and not wanting to cough in his customer's face.

Herb would cut his eyes at him and the message would be delivered without words. Herb would never have said anything in front of the customers. The cat used to get so stoned that by five o'clock he couldn't cut another head and Herb would tell him to go home. He'd come back the next morning apologizing and promising never to do it again. And always Herb would forgive him.

Things went on like that for a year until Herb finally had to let him go. The cat went up and down the street telling everybody what a rotten bastard Herb was for kicking him out after the way he had run the shop so efficiently for him and all and the way he used to stay late and see to it that Herb could get away for other business. Then he made up a lie about how tight Herb was for not giving him what he was really worth. That was a lie and everybody should have known it. But you know what? People believed this guy—some of them *actually believed* him. It's convenient to believe only what you want to believe, though, isn't it?

Sometimes a singer who had made it up the ladder to one of the big clubs downtown would come in and tell stories of things that had happened to him in Detroit and New York and Philadelphia and San Francisco. Everyone would sit quietly through each tale and then prime him for another. Black Jack kept us posted on who had hit the numbers and for how much and Stick and Big P. would argue about who had the best girls. Cats would come in selling hot shoes and shirts and socks and jackets and coats and furs and cufflinks and all kinds of good buys.

Sometimes Red Top and I would buy, but mostly we'd just look the crap over and pass it on to the next cat, who would look it over and pass it on to the next, who would look it over . . . And somebody was always stopping in to put the quiet touch on Herb. They'd come in and whisper something in his ear, he'd nod and run his hand in his pocket and bring out the right amount. He had a knack for bringing out just what the guy had asked for and no more, and he'd nonchalantly slide it into the cat's hand with his left hand while his right hand kept cutting and cutting and cutting.

And the slick-'em-back boys would sit under the dryers with their scalps tingling and their inner souls bursting with anticipation, and longing for the waves to be meticulously set by the barber, who has grown to be barber-beautician with the advent of the new hair-straightening operation called "The Process." Now the whole *world* can have straight hair.

We'd get our monthly haircut and sit around for another hour or two soaking up the stories and then we'd cut out for Jake's Lounge and sit for a while drinking whiskey and beer and then drop by the Cut-Rate Liquor Store for the stockpile of wine. We'd take the blood home and hide it from ourselves and then take off for the street with a pint in the back pocket, off for the big street, stopping in alleys from time to time to taste. . . . Up and down the street, one side and the other, pinching butts, joking, making out, trying to make out (but you've always got to pay) the best we knew how and sharing wine with the cats who didn't have any because they'd have some sooner or later and we damn sure wanted to be on the list when they started paying back. And as always we'd get damn good and drunk and end up with some of the reserve supply gone and a babe in the bed who's still drunk. She had to be drunk when you woke up or it didn't seem real. If you got one who was as sober as you the next morning you didn't trust her; you just knew she had taken all of the blood and hid it someplace while you were stoned. You'd wake her up and send her off to continue her hustle, and start Tuesday off with a tall glass of ice-cold water, trying to activate the high and get it going again without drinking any of your blood. It never worked, though, so you'd have to start in again in order to remain stable and steady.

the street

The Street was dead in the morning and afternoon. Everybody there was a drag—the squares at work and their square bosses and the real ultra-square snobs who shopped in the uprated stores and paid the price of having the store close at hand and paid the price of buying from Mr. Honest, who would uprate the price on his mother or even God himself. . . . Man, it was like a different street in the daytime, but without the el running overhead it would have been nothing.

The Street itself, excluding the businesses and the el tracks overhead, is old and in rotten shape. A million years ago streetcars used to crawl back and forth in front of the businesses and then they killed all the red beauties and replaced them with buses and found they had to cover over the tracks to increase the life of the buses. The work crews came through with big grotesque machines and poured a thin layer of asphalt over the tracks.

That was a million years ago. Now the tracks are coming through, shiny and silvery; coming through the black blacktop. There are long narrow cracks running from curb to curb. There are holes in the street and the curbs are peeling away. Little children come along and pick up pieces of the street and throw them at buses and at cars and at each other.

The holes are getting bigger! The street is caving in. A car fell in and disappeared! *They* want the Street to disappear; the businesses and people, *they* want them all to fall in the holes and never come out. *They* can't handle the problem and *they* want to go to sleep one night and wake up the next morning and find the Street gone forever. And then *they* can build a new street for a new people.

The way it stands now, the Street, it begins at a point I like to call the beginning and runs to the end, but I'm only concerned about three blocks—no, I'm concerned about four blocks. It begins with the drugstore and coming this way from the drugstore on this side of the Street the businesses go like this: a storefront church and a tavern next and then a barbecue place and a Chinese laundry followed by a greasy spoon where the food stinks but still tastes good; then a jewelry store, a shoestore, a tavern, a record shop that fronts for the biggest policy wheel in the neighborhood, then a church (the preacher plays the numbers every day except Sunday), then a poolroom and another liquor store and then a pawnshop and a house with a lot of women where men come and go from sundown to sunup, and straight on down the Street like that for another few blocks. The other side of the Street seems to be about the same way, except I think there are *more* taverns over there.

And the hotel, I forgot the hotel! The Place of Peace Hotel. It isn't really on the Street. It's around the corner in the middle of the block. It's not right to mention the Street without paying equal homage to the Place of Peace Hotel because that's where Red Top and I live, along with many of the other gentlemen of independent means. It's nice that way because there's a feeling of real equality. Well, usually there's a feeling of equality. You see, once in a while somebody's check is lost or stolen and they have to run downtown, fill out all kinds of papers and then wait a few more days before it arrives in the mail. It happened to me a couple of times and believe me, you feel pretty left out—like there's no justice in the world.

The elevated runs over the Street twenty-four hours a day. At night it sends millions of little sparks glowing weird colors that never reach the ground. In daylight the elevated structure helps to shade the Street, but thin lines of sunlight creep through the spaces between the ties and stamp the sidewalk with their warming message. The structure is strong now but someday they'll tire of it and say it's ugly and must come down. And that will be the end of the Street.

The elevated turns north about one-half mile from our little nest and slides smoothly along the tracks to another world. Red Top and I traveled the full distance one day. We went from our little World of Nothing to a world of even less. I guess that's the only way to describe their world: a World of Even Less. It doesn't seem right that a people can have so much and still have nothing. We could show them but they don't want any part of us so we'll just keep it to ourselves and have something of real substance from practically nothing of value.

This city being divided up into little neighborhoods the way it is, it's interesting to see people of like customs getting on at the same stop. And even more interesting to see the people from a different neighborhood look down their noses at them. It's a strange city: the Irish hate the Poles; the Poles hate the Italians; the Italians hate the Germans; the Germans hate the Puerto Ricans; the Puerto Ricans hate the Spaniards; the Spaniards hate the Jews and they all join together to hate the blacks. It's a good God-fearing city.

The elevated streaks along through the city of hate—through the fat dirty melting pot that never seems to jell; through the unassimilated groups of monsters clawing their way to the top of the pot; through the millions of people who conform to a pattern of life because it's too difficult to think, it's too costly to be oneself; through millions of sheep following the lead sheep over the side of a cliff!

I said it was interesting to see these people and it is, but it is also frightening. It is frightening as hell to think that sooner or later Nothing, too, will be swept into this whirling hysteria and its life will be supplanted by slogans and gadgets and hate. I hope I'm not around when it goes.

Red Top and I got off the train after our ride and tried to forget the burning hate-eyes that stared at us and through us with a few quick sips of the joy juice. We may be nothing but thank God we're not advanced enough to be machines.

silky martin, retired wheel

Red Top and I used to have so much fun together. We'd leave the barbershop and hang around the poolroom until it got dark. And when the sun went down and the fluorescent lights started winking at each other up and down the Street and everybody came out in the open, things that had been dead for hours came to life and the party was on again. We did have fun.

There was a rib joint on the corner that had a specially treated charcoal that smelled better than all the other barbecue houses in the world. Silky Martin owned the place along with a few taverns and even more apartment buildings he bought with the money he had made from his policy wheel before the syndicate and Feds moved in on him. Silky's an old man now, gray and round, but he still carries himself as if he's ready to take on the world—everybody but the syndicate and Feds. He wants no part of them. He runs a little book from his seat behind the cash register. I guess the book is more trouble than it's worth, but he's happy with it. I asked him why he bothered since he had so few bets these days. He said it's so he can keep in touch with the boys. But the boys don't need him. They don't want him. They proved that when they robbed him of his wheel. It's terrible to want to belong and have nobody want you—and the boys don't want Silky.

For a long time after the boys took over Silky's policy wheel, Silky wouldn't tolerate discussions about who hit on what number, but within the year his anxiety had possessed him and he resorted to paying winos to bet for him just so he could see the little thin policy slips. Sometimes we could see him behind the cash register caressing the slips and staring out the window and through the whole world; back to a world that he loved and missed and wanted.

Silky didn't like using the winos to bet for him, but he didn't want to be seen talking to a policy runner who worked for the syndicate that stole his empire, so even though he knew that he could never expect to see any winnings if he was fortunate enough to pick the right number, because everybody knows you can't trust a wino (even Silky knew this), he was still willing to bet through them because the children of the grape were the only ones who would run the errands and remain silent about it. They would never humiliate him by reminding him that he was a has-been. They would never make fun of the old man living in the pre-syndicate days. They would never talk of the dead man as his friends did; dead and afraid. They would never talk so long as he contributed toward the magic pint. . . . It's like I've always said: I'm glad I'm not a wino because that's bad. I drink the stuff in fairly substantial quantities, but I'm not a wino.

Aside from the convenience of the book and the joy of associating with an ex-wheel, there is the fact that Silky's ribs are the best in the world, and Red Top and I used to make it a point to eat there at least twice a week. Even the cole slaw and bread had a distinctive taste that was peculiar to Silky's place. All the guys from the Street met there. If we weren't in a position to buy, we would mooch. If we couldn't mooch enough for a meal, we would beg a bone or a taste of slaw. And though sometimes we'd go home empty inside, no bone, no slaw, no bread, we were still filled with the vivid memory of the gleaming coals smoking and cooking the best ribs in the world and the joy of having been in the company of Silky Martin, retired wheel afraid of the syndicate and the Feds.

miss joanne joanne smiles down on junkie thaddeus popcorn jones

Two years ago Miss Joanne Joanne met a young man. Must tell you about Miss Joanne Joanne and her warm message of friendship.

To begin with, Miss Joanne Joanne was the madam's prize protégée (the madam of the house I told you about—you know, the one with all the women where the men come and go, etc.), brought along slowly for four years. At the age of twenty she was quick, but not so quick as to rush the patrons. Next to the madam, Joanne Joanne was the wealthiest woman in the neighborhood. She had tiny feet and straight narrow calves that seemed rather inadequate as supports for the full, round torso resting on them. She had small delicate hands, long hair, long eyelashes and a long neck and even a long head. But she was beautiful. She was a doll. She was gentle and friendly and kind to drunks and animals. She hated junkies, though. Like this was the one moral conviction she had and she wasn't about to let it slip away from her. She couldn't stand to be on the same street with a junkie.

As proof of her convictions, she once pushed a junkie in front of a car. That was Junkie Thaddeus Popcorn Jones. She did it because he stopped her on the street one afternoon and asked for a nickel to get a candy bar—*right* in the path of a bright shiny Cadillac, *wham!*

Of course the car knocked the hell out of Junkie Thaddeus Popcorn Jones and bounced him all the way across the street. This didn't bother Miss Joanne Joanne, though; she wasn't the least bit upset; she just continued on her walk and tried to forget that the lowest animal in the world had spoken to her. She was furious for weeks. And then she finally forgot about it until one day a few months later a dapper young man called on her at the house and said he just wanted to talk and was willing to pay by the minute for her conversation. They talked.

They talked for two hours and then the young man got up to leave and thanked her for talking with him and thanked her for being gentle and kind and thanked her for making it possible for him to make five thousand dollars for nothing.

It seems that the driver of the automobile didn't see Miss Joanne Joanne push Junkie Thaddeus Popcorn Jones into the street. And it seems that the driver was drunk and a man of some social position with excellent insurance. Only a junkie can be so lucky. The police were slow in arriving on the scene of the accident and a chaser for a personal-injury lawyer downtown got there first, lined up three or four witnesses, told them what they were to say they had seen, washed Junkie Thaddeus Popcorn Jones's face, combed his hair, slipped his own sport coat on over the dirty shirt Junkie Thaddeus Popcorn Jones had worn for several months, inserted five five-dollar bills in his pocket so he would be more than just another derelict, bribed the noble police officer to write a mountain of tickets and give the driver a drunkometer test and had the poor, helpless victim transported to a small hospital owned by a doctor who worked in close association with the chaser's employer, where the medical bills could grow and grow and grow under the trained eyes of a personal-injury specialist.

The junkie had spent three months in a private room with a radio, a television set, all he could eat and once in a while a fix—because of pain, of course.

And now he had come back to thank Miss Joanne Joanne after getting his settlement with three thousand dollars clear, a new wardrobe and a warm place in his heart for the lovely Miss Joanne Joanne. He had to see her before he did anything else because he had big plans for the money.

He was going to pay his rent for the coming year. He was going to invest one thousand five hundred dollars in a combination poolroom–chicken shack and put it in the hands of a member of his family, who would operate it and guarantee that the business would remain on a paying basis. And then he was going to bargain with his pusher like he had never bargained before and buy enough junk to keep every one of his junkie friends high for at least six months. That is, all those who didn't die from hot shots.

Miss Joanne Joanne was so upset she had to take a vacation to quiet her nerves. Word travels fast down here, and the young man, Junkie Thaddeus Popcorn Jones, was famous for being the man who said, "Thanks to you, I can get the whole world high."

never vote only once (or how to vote in chicago)

We had a primary election last year. Red Top and I voted five times at two dollars a vote. Five names, five addresses—it gets pretty confusing some years, especially when we vote in the really big elections and vote ten or fifteen times. I guess people might think we're pretty foul citizens for selling our votes the way we do, but in the final analysis it all comes out the same. After all, we're really not selling our votes; it's more like being paid to protect ourselves. That's right. It's common sense. Look, the people who make it possible for us to stay in our welfare state can't continue to shower us with our tiny monthly checks if we don't make damn sure they stay in office. It's sort of a reciprocal trade agreement we have. They keep us fat and happy and we keep them fatter and happier.

Personally, I don't see any difference between us out here in Nothing voting to keep what we have and those other people on the other side voting to make damn sure we don't get what they have. It's all the same to me—it's purely a matter of doing what we're told to do by those in charge so they can stay in charge. There is one difference, however, and that is that we not only get paid all year but get an added bonus on election day.

Now I know many people don't like what we do every year on election day, but we can't help ourselves. Honest. We've got orders.

The precinct captain makes it quite clear every year. He gets us all together and says: "Now this year I'm expecting you guys to carry me over the hump. We been takin' care of you bastards all year and you better be sober enough to vote next week. . . . And if I so much as hear that one of you stops voting before my assistants tell you to, I'll have your ass. You'll be told where to go and when they tell you to vote I expect you to vote and vote and vote and . . ."

See what I mean? They've got us the way they want us. One of these years, though, if they let me, I'll make fifty dollars.

frenchy coolbreeze, virtuoso supreme

Every so often a new musician appears in the hotel. These musicians come from all over the country to this, the jazz center of the universe, equipped only with their instruments and dreams of a quick rise to success. Once in a while one of them makes it and hundreds of dreamers follow hoping to repeat the magical process of their predecessors.

Frenchy Coolbreeze was such a man. He came to Chicago with his expensive French horn, a little talent and a million dreams. Frenchy was muscular for a musician (more like a weight lifter), about five feet eleven and weighed two hundred pounds. He looked funny wrapped around his tiny French horn.

We saw him the day he arrived in Chicago. He came in a car—a new one at that—with a Minnesota license plate. He parked just a few cars away from the entrance, fumbled around in the back for a while, then stepped out of the car carrying a French horn under one arm and a thick stack of records under the other.

Right then and there we knew he was a musician to be reckoned with.

Frenchy was not one to go out of his way to make friends; he was not one to stand on the corner with the rest of us and tell jokes and lies and flirt and try to pick up something for no more than the price of a little conversation—he was a French horn virtuoso and determined to take his place in the annals of jazz as the supreme leader of a new school. He blew mellow, easy-flowing phrases that tied together in a pleasant continuing sound—always miles behind the beat. That was the effect he wanted. Like the great Lester Young, he was going to come along after everybody else with something worth hearing. There was only one thing wrong with Mr. Frenchy Coolbreeze: he was so cool he forgot that jazz has to have a beat; without it, it just ain't jazz. Well, maybe I'm not being fair about Frenchy. I think I'll say that, coming from a white society somewhere in Minnesota, he had not learned what jazz really was and came to Chicago to find soul.

Frenchy also had another reason for coming to the windy city: to do battle with the saxophone. He felt the saxophone was a bastard instrument and didn't belong anywhere—surely not in a jazz band. He was devoted to his instrument and determined to prove its superiority.

During those first few months before summer the hotel was filled with the haunting sounds of an instrument that was completely new to us. We didn't like it, but since most of us owed Frenchy money, it was not our place to object.

In time the weather broke and the days and nights

were hot and humid. The windows were open in every apartment in every building and Frenchy Coolbreeze played all night, to the satisfaction or dissatisfaction of the residents of the block. Next door to the hotel the bass player (a swinging young man named Hardy Jones) would hear Frenchy Coolbreeze sliding along from phrase to phrase, pick up his bow and blend in with a new sound to accompany the French horn. And out in the street a teen-ager who carried a pair of drumsticks in his back pocket would keep the beat even while playing on an automobile or a light pole or a cardboard box or perhaps a garbage can.

Now across the street there was an alto saxophone man named Randolph Beard. Randy usually practiced in the afternoon when he got home from work. He was having some difficulty sleeping with the French horn, bass and drum going most of the night and he decided to go to bed as soon as he got home, get up at midnight and blast Frenchy Coolbreeze back to Minnesota. He had heard some of the things Frenchy was supposed to have said about the horn he loved and he welcomed this chance to put the young punk in his place. Besides, he didn't like the idea, he said, "of some nut with one of those symphony orchestra instruments trying to sound like a pure jazz instrument."

The duel between horns began Sunday night at eleven-fifty-nine and lasted until the sun came up. Early the next morning betting began. During the day odds shifted from one side to the other and by ten o'clock Monday night the odds were five to three that Frenchy Coolbreeze could not possibly hold out another night.

But he did. When the sun came up Tuesday morning

they were still battling and by mutual agreement they decided to terminate the duel until the following night. The money went back to the gamblers and betting began all over again.

That night something new had come to the block and the duel took on a new perspective. Word of the duel between the old school and the new traveled throughout the city and by eleven o'clock there were no fewer than twenty-five musicians waiting to pass judgment on the quality of playing rather than on physical endurance.

At exactly eleven-fifty-nine Frenchy Coolbreeze sat on his windowsill with one leg out the window and the other braced against the frame. He bowed to the judges below and began to play. He blew for thirty minutes and when he finished the judges applauded and cheered for fifteen minutes. Frenchy Coolbreeze had learned to play jazz. Of course the judges were all of the new cool school and they understood his playing even if we didn't.

The block became quiet again and the judges waited for Randy to make his appearance. He did not come out.

Someone shouted, "I say we make Frenchy the winner."

The crowd cheered and began applauding again.

Frenchy held his horn high over his head to acknowledge the applause. It was then that the shot rang out through the night. *Ka-rang!* And the shiny French horn was seen flying through the air.

With this the duel had officially ended and Frenchy Coolbreeze was indeed a virtuoso supreme.

cadillac bill rides on

Cadillac Bill was one of those rare creatures who become a legend during their lifetime. He was very tall, very handsome, very adept at surviving by various means of hustling and very apt to tell lie after lie about the days when money was good and plentiful and he didn't have a wife and three children to feed and he was the best car thief in the world. The legend of Cadillac Bill probably came into being because it's the nature of man to make a story a little better than the way it was originally told. Cadillac Bill had been telling stories about the Cadillac cars he used to steal for ten or fifteen years. These same stories have been told again and again by his friends as they stand on the street passing the bottle around and swapping tales. And as the men get drunker the stories grow more meaningful, but further from the truth.

Now one whole generation of children in the World of Nothing has come of age and has lived with these stories for so long that the lies have become truth and Cadillac Bill is truly the greatest Cadillac car stealer in the world.

It was a warm day in July when one of our younger

men, newly knighted to manhood, was partaking in the before-noon sip and describing in precise detail the artistic operation of Cadillac Bill.

You see, there's a strange thing about stories. We've learned to never doubt a story when it's being told because if you don't believe in the story you kill it—it can't be true. But if you only pretend to doubt it and you really believe the story, then you have the makings of a great tale, then you have a true story.

We were pretending to doubt the story when Cadillac Bill drove up in his shiny new red Chevy convertible. He parked his car and came to join us.

The young man was crushed by the car he saw. "Hey, Cadillac Bill. What the hell you doin' with that little car?"

"It's a long story. It's a long story, boy. I got a wife and kids now."

"Yeah, but a Chevy. You in a Chevy. I mean, Cadillac Bill, it just ain't right that you have to suffer like this. It just ain't fair that you of all people can't have a Cadillac car in your old days—I don't mean old days, but when you a mature man. We just ought to get you a Cadillac car."

"You know somethin', son, you really right about that. You really right. I always had a Cadillac car. You guys want to know somethin'? I always had a Cadillac car. I had my first one when I was twelve years old. And you know somethin' about that car?" He laughed and slapped the young man on the back and the young man laughed out of respect. "My old man took it from me and went drivin' around like he owned it and the police caught him and he got ninety days."

When we stopped laughing, the young man said, "Hey, Cadillac Bill, remember the time you stole ten Cadillacs in one day and parked them all in front of the police station?"

Cadillac Bill looked at the faces around him, sizing up the audience. Everybody knows if you believe what you're saying it can't be a lie and Cadillac Bill looked like he was trying to believe it. He turned to the young man and said, "Son, I think it was nine."

"No, no. It was ten. I know it was ten because I was just a little punk and you took me with you and when we got it you said, 'Boy, this is number ten for today.' And we took that old Cadillac and parked it right in front of the police station. Ain't that right, now? Ain't that the way it really was?"

"Now that you mention it, I guess it was ten at that. Seems to me I set some kind of record that day."

"That's right. You sure did. And remember the time you stole a Cadillac car to drive in a funeral?"

"That's the time I had a police escort, son. I'd have to remember that."

"Yeah, that's one time you got caught."

"Wait a minute, now. I was never caught for stealin' a car. The only time I ever got caught was when I went out of my field into somethin' I didn't know about."

We all agreed that Cadillac Bill had never been convicted of stealing a car. We passed the bottle around again and waited for the tale to grow another limb.

"Well," the young man said, wine dripping from his lower lip, "I know one thing for sure—you ain't suppose to be around here drivin' nothin' but a Cadillac. It just ain't right, with your reputation and all, that you can't have one now. In fact, if we suppose to be such good friends of yours, we sure ought to keep you supplied with the kind of car you deserve. And that's just what I'm gonna do. I'm gonna get you a pretty white Cadillac. I know where one is you'll like. You wait right here."

"Now wait a minute, son. I'm not sayin' I don't appreciate what you want to do for me, but you see, I'm—"

"I know you do, Cadillac, and I know you want me to be careful. And I will." The young man started down the block with two of his younger friends. "Don't forget, Cadillac Bill," he called back, "everything I know I learned from you, so you know I'll be all right."

Cadillac Bill was unsteady but he had to keep up the front. "Hurry back," he called out, his voice trembling just a bit.

We knew he had been forced into waiting. Even if the young man wasn't his pupil, he had said he was and we believed it, and that made it so. Cadillac Bill had to wait and sweat it out just like the young man was sweating it out to prove himself.

We passed the bottle (a new one by now) and swapped stories about the big war and France and England and women the world over. Within the hour the young man returned, blowing the horn of a flashy white Cadillac convertible.

"Hop in, Cadillac. It's all yours."

Cadillac Bill drove around the block twenty-five times before he turned the car back over to the young man with careful instructions on how to dispose of it. Cadillac Bill watched the young man drive away; then he turned to us and said, "That's the only kind of car a man should have. I just might buy myself one some one of these days."

We didn't see the young man again for six months. As the story goes, he was arrested in front of the police station.

miss luhester gives a party

Luhester Homan owned a frame bungalow a few doors south of the hotel. She was one of the most highly respected ladies in the neighborhood. She was five feet two inches tall and would have been considered to be not quite but almost plump. Her hair was dark brown, of course, and she was a nice even walnut without the slightest imperfection anywhere on her lovely smooth skin. She was a happy woman and had enough love for her five children and everyone in the world. She always had a kind word and a pleasant smile for people she passed on the street.

Luhester had never bothered to get married and she was therefore supported by the county. And since all of the men loved her so, they felt personally responsible for each of the five children. Hers was an attractive group of children, but I'm afraid they didn't favor each other very much. However, they did all seem to have some of Luhester in them and she loved all of them equally.

The fellows in the neighborhood sort of looked after Luhester. It wasn't at all unusual to see two or three of us carrying packages of clothing every first of the month on our way to Luhester's house. The paternal instinct was so strong in all of us that we were determined that Luhester's children would be the best dressed in the neighborhood. And they were.

There was a garage at the rear of Luhester's house and Mr. Beckman, the owner of the local hardware store, stored his supplies in this garage behind four locks and five steel bars. Quite often he worked late moving supplies from the garage to the store, and before he went home to his wife and children he stopped by to visit with Luhester. He was a good man. She was the kind of person you just automatically wanted to protect and Mr. Beckman began storing his supplies in her garage just because he wanted to help her earn enough money to afford some of the necessaries of life. As a result of his kindness, hers was the best maintained house on the block and always open for company. That is, unless Mr. Beckman was there. We didn't want to disturb him because he was such a good man.

Red Top and I passed her place one day and saw her standing on a ladder painting the trim. She was having a pretty hard time of it because the baby girl was awake and kept crying. Luhester would have to get down off the ladder and run inside to see if little Jo Jo was all right. We watched her for a while, running into the house and then walking back out, climbing the ladder, making a few strokes with the brush, then down off the ladder again and back into the house. Seeing her in such a troubled condition made us both a little uneasy so we took over the painting chores. She affected everyone about the same way. We finished the trim that first day and went on the next morning, after eating a healthy breakfast she had prepared for us, and did both porches.

Somebody else pitched in a few days later and finished the rest of the house. That spring the whole house was painted inside and out. It was probably the only house ever painted out of love.

As a token of her appreciation, Luhester gave a party for the kind men of the community. We were in the poolroom one evening at about seven o'clock sitting around watching Stick clean some sucker of all his money, when Luhester's oldest daughter, Little Luhester, came in and invited the chosen few with her sweet young voice whispering in our ears. "Mama says you suppose to come right away for the party."

Now the word "party" has different meanings to different people, but everyone knows it means fun. When Little Luhester pulled Stick's hand away from his cue, stood on her toes and whispered the magic words in his ear, it was like the voice of providence telling him to end the game immediately and hurry to the party. He couldn't miss the party because everybody knows it's really bad luck to miss a party, especially a party you're invited to attend. Stick took the omen for what it was worth and finished the game by running the last six balls off the table and banking the eight ball three-in-the-side. He had been carrying the sucker along, beating him by only one or two balls each time. But he couldn't take the chance of ruining his luck by missing the party so he had to bring the game to an end and be happy with the eight dollars he had already won.

Jesse, too, knew the punishment for missing a party, and when Little Luhester passed the message on to him he got down from his creaky stool and started turning off lights at the rear of the room.

"Okay. That's it for today. I'm closin' up early."

"What the hell you mean," Cadillac Bill said. "I just started my game."

"Finish it tomorrow."

"Tomorrow, hell! I paid my money and I'll play the game."

Just then the bearer of sweet words whispered the same magic to Cadillac Bill.

"Well," Cadillac said to Jesse, "if you gotta close, you gotta close."

When Little Luhester left the poolroom, everyone who was to be invited had been contacted and no one wanted to let it be known that there was a party for fear that the uninvited would string along and spoil the magic before it had a chance to work. Fat Man had not been invited and he wondered where everyone was hurrying to so suddenly.

"Hey, Stick," Fat Man said, "where y'all goin'?"

"I'm just headin' home, man. Ain't none of yo' business where I go noway. Why you always think somebody's goin' someplace? Why don't you go on home and stop bothering people?"

With that, Fat Man knew there were pleasant happenings in the area. He left the poolroom and waited in the dark to follow Stick to the festivities.

The party was a tremendous success. Luhester had been buying two gallons of wine a month for five months, planning just such an occasion as this as the time for the unscrewing of the caps. She had made potato salad and sweet potatoes and black-eyed peas and baked a ham and fried four chickens. She had her Catholic Salvage hi-fi going full blast when two girls who worked at Silky Martin's came in, kicked off their shoes, helped themselves to some of the wine and started dancing.

Frenchy Coolbreeze and Randolph Beard sat at opposite corners of the room staring at each other for the first hour. By the second hour they had forgotten their anger and laughed loudly about their duel. By the third hour each was proclaiming the other the world's most gifted musician. But then Stick asked Randy if he still had the high-powered rifle he had brought home from Germany and Frenchy Coolbreeze returned to his corner and continued staring through the rest of the party.

Cadillac Bill was busy following Luhester around, rubbing her stomach and saying, "Magic stomach, magic stomach, bring me a little baby Cadillac."

One of the girls went upstairs with Red Top and stayed for about forty-five minutes.

Junkie Thaddeus Popcorn Jones drank a glass of wine and vomited in the potato salad.

Stick tried to pull Luhester upstairs but she fought him off successfully without damaging their friendship.

Tommie Murphy watered the flowers with wine.

The girl went back upstairs with Red Top. Red Top

came down alone. The girl followed fifteen minutes later with Cadillac Bill.

Fat Man didn't crash the party until we were all feeling pretty good and by then it didn't matter. Miss Joanne Joanne arrived at exactly eleven o'clock with a bottle of bourbon for the hostess, saw two junkies sleeping in the corner and left.

By midnight Doc (the drugstore janitor) and Cadillac Bill had gotten into three fights; each of them swearing that Little Luhester was his daughter. After we stopped the last fight and they cooled off, they confessed a deep lasting love for Luhester.

These magic parties either go on until morning or end abruptly because some mysterious chain of events wills it so. This grand party could not last all night because parties that linger on to the predawn hours lose their magic when the sun comes up. Everyone knows a party has to end before morning to be a success.

Silky Martin got up from his chair to leave and nudged Fat Man, who was standing over Stick. Stick was wearing his new sport jacket—a soft gold with green stripes. When he realized that Fat Man had spilled a glass of wine on him, he jumped to his feet and with one punch knocked Fat Man through the living room window onto the porch. Luhester had gone upstairs hours before this with Doc and they had no idea that downstairs Fat Man and Stick were methodically breaking up every piece of furniture in the living room. The two girls left but got their dresses slightly torn as they tried to break away from Red Top and Tommie Murphy. Silky Martin had eased out without anyone discovering that he had started things going, and the winos from the corner left. Of course they left—the food and wine were all gone. Things were really going good, so I gathered the few records I had brought, along with some of those Frenchy Coolbreeze had brought, and went home to bed.

The magic had worked; the party was the best we ever had.

the hot shot

Sometimes Red Top and I wake up and look at each other and know instantly that the whole day will be a big fat bust. We've got this thing going between us and we know there's nothing to do but get stoned some way —and fast. I guess it's what we call the blues or the burns or the drags. That's it. It's the drags. I mean, it's just a drag to have to wake up feeling that way. Like no matter what you do the whole day, forget it; if you don't get stoned there's no way out of it. Otherwise, you'll feel like hell and you'll hit out to the Street and the next thing you know you'll be in a fight and end up cut or cutting somebody and then you've got to leave town for a few days until they forget they're supposed to be looking for you. See, the drags just lead you right into further drags if you don't check them; and the only way to check them is to get drunk and stay that way until the next day. The drags never last any more than one day at a time.

Red Top and I had the drags like that once and it was a terrible case. That was the first time we tried H. That was the only time we tried H. Heroin is for fools and we were fools that day, but we had the drags so bad we had to do something and since it was offered to us on a freebie we couldn't turn it down.

Tommie Murphy had worked for a week pressing clothes in the cleaners when their regular presser went out on strike. Tommie spent his entire week's salary on H. It's funny how we met him. Probably won't happen again for at least six years.

We woke up this morning with the drags. Red Top looked at me and I looked at him and we knew we had the drags. There was no need for words. We got dressed, walked downstairs and sat on the steps trying to clear our heads. It was a beautiful morning but that didn't make things any better. It had rained the night before and the sidewalks were clean and the air smelled sweet and green. It was quiet in front of the hotel except for a few children pushing sticks around the puddles of water at the curb. The clouds broke and the sun began drying the sidewalks and the street, but we couldn't appreciate it—we had the drags bad and there was only one way out.

We decided we weren't going to buy pints this day because it would take too many, so we agreed to buy three quarts of wine each and go back to the apartment and get stoned in the peaceful quiet of our rooms while lying in our cots looking out the window at the kids.

We got right up to the Cut-Rate Liquor Store when Tommie Murphy came running down the street with four pairs of pressed khakis draped over his arm. He saw us and called Red Top over to the side and whispered something to him. Red Top frowned for a few seconds, then his face lit up like he was his own sun and he came over to me and whispered in my ear: "He wants to give us some H. I'm for it if you are."

I thought about it awhile and it didn't sound too good; besides, I couldn't think too clearly. I had the drags and I was torn between a high I knew and a high I had to know sooner or later.

Tommie grabbed my arm and said, "Look, man, one time ain't gonna hook you. One time ain't gonna hurt you and it ain't gonna make you a junkie, but it *is* gonna make you high, baby, the best high in the world."

I still wasn't sure. I didn't like the idea. I didn't even like Tommie, for that matter. He was a junkie and you can't trust junkies. The only reason why he wanted to get us high is because he knew it wouldn't take much for us since we weren't users in the first place and then after it was over he could brag about how big he was because he got two cats high when he had the big batch he bought with the money he worked so hard to get. Actually I believed that he just wanted to get us hooked on the shit like he was. I didn't like Tommie.

"Tell you what," Red Top said to me. "Let's get some wine first and then we can shoot the stuff after that. See, Tommie," he said, turning away from me, "we ain't had nothin' to eat so this can make it for breakfast."

We agreed. I guess I felt I could get my guts from

the wine and it wouldn't matter what I did after I had had a couple of swallows burning down in my stomach. I bought the wine and three bags of potato chips and we finished it off on our way to Alonzo Hit-Man Smith's house.

Hit-Man Smith was a smooth, steady hand and could find a vein on an ant. He had been a medic in the army during the war and came out using a needle like an M.D. He had a basement flat a couple of blocks away (I forget the number now), and he had rugs on all the floors and more furniture than he would need in three lives. You see, Hit-Man was a pusher, too, and when a junkie needed a fix bad and didn't have money, he'd find someplace to pick up something he knew Hit-Man would like and bring it over and offer it in return for a fix.

Hit-Man had an Oriental rug in his living room that must have gone for at least a thousand dollars. A junkie stole it from a department store downtown in broad daylight. He was a brave junkie. He put on a pair of coveralls, rode downtown on the bus, walked into the store, bent over, rolled the rug up into a nice tight roll, took two pieces of string from his pocket, tied the rug at both ends, walked to the rear of the store, out the service entrance onto the street, down in the subway and straight to Hit-Man's house. Junkies are luckier than winos because they're crazy.

When we got to Hit-Man's house, Tommie kicked on the door and called him. "Hit-Man! Hit-Man! Open the door, Hit-Man. Hit-Man! I got us some more, Hit-Man, so open the door."

The door opened and Hit-Man stood in the doorway,

a big, muscular, ugly man in fur-lined slippers, pajamas and a silk robe. "Come in. Come in, Tommie Tiger. Bring your friends in and we'll have some coffee and sweet rolls. By the way, wipe your feet good, will you? I don't want to get my rugs dirty."

"Sure, Hit-Man," Tommie said. "Sure, we'll wipe 'em good. Come on, you guys, let's make it."

Inside, Tommie took the khakis off his arm and handed them to Hit-Man, who placed them on a hanger and hung them in the hall closet, handling them delicately as if they were worth something, with his thumb and forefinger holding the hanger; his thick forefinger and thumb, manicured stumps, polished lobster claws clamped down on a fragile piece of metal. Then Tommie reached into his pocket and came out with a tobacco pouch. He unzipped the pouch, inserted three fingers and gently extracted a piece of tissue paper and held it out in front of him so we could all see the white paper folded over the white junk.

Tommie smiled at the Hit-Man and the Hit-Man returned his smile. Tommie smiled at Red Top and Red Top returned his smile. Tommie smiled at me and I laughed. The ceremony was funny as hell. I thought he was getting ready to give us all communion. Hit-Man motioned to the kitchen and Tommie started walking slowly, very slowly, in that direction. Hit-Man followed him and I followed Hit-Man and Red Top followed me.

Hit-Man took a slicing board from the cupboard, placed it on the table and beamed as Tommie gently placed the paper in the center of the board. Then Hit-Man went to work. He filled two pots with water and placed them on the stove. He then took a flashlight from the shelf of the cupboard, a sterling silver concave disk and a pair of forceps. The forceps he deposited in one pot. Next he unscrewed the bottom of the flashlight and emptied out a syringe, a small burner and a half-dozen or so needles. He then put the syringe and four of the needles in the other pot.

Tommie was impatient. "Look, Hit-Man," he said, "do we have to go through all this medical jazz today?"

Hit-Man turned the hot water on and started washing his hands. "Tommie, I have a reputation. I do things the way they should be done. When I was in the army the doctors used to say I was the only person who never broke sterile technique. You wouldn't want me to change my ways now, would you, just because you're too anxious? You know why everybody comes to me. They come to me because I do things right. Everything I do I do right. Now just be patient. Help yourself to some of those sweet rolls in the breadbox while I scrub in. By the way, how much of that H is mine?"

"What the hell you mean?" Tommie said. "I'm gettin' you high, ain't I? That's all you get—just enough for a fix and no more."

"Tommie, my good boy, I merely want to put some of it up so you'll be able to get high tomorrow."

"I'm not leavin' here till it's all gone. I figure we got enough for two days."

"Who'd you get it from, Tommie?"

"You don't know him. No need worryin' about it, 'cause you don't know him."

"You know, I should be hurt. You could have bought it from me."

"I know, Hit-Man, but I been wantin' some straight stuff for a long time and yours ain't straight."

"Of course it is, Tommie. I don't cut mine any more than the rest of the guys. It's as straight as you'll get anywhere in town."

"The hell it is."

"Tell you what," Hit-Man said, rinsing and lathering his hands again. "I won't argue with you. It's too nice a day and you are company, so I'll forgive you this time."

"Thanks, Hit-Man. You know how it is. This is suppose to be pure, man, pure! Everybody ought to have some pure stuff at least once in a lifetime."

Hit-Man turned the water off with his elbow. "We'll soon find out," he said. He walked to the stove holding his hands up like a surgeon, and stood looking at the instruments bouncing around in the boiling water while we ate all of his sweet rolls and helped ourselves to a few Cokes. He turned off the stove, elbows again, and said, "Tommie, take the pot holder and empty the water out of this one. Be careful not to let the forceps fall out of the pot, and then turn the burner off under the other pot and set the cooker up, please."

Tommie poured the water out and put the pot back on the stove.

"Now as soon as it's cool enough to touch," Hit-Man said, "I'll reach in with my fingers and take the forceps out and we're in business. This isn't really the way it's supposed to be done, but I don't have gloves so this will have to do. If somebody could get me a little autoclave I'd be able to sterilize everything in that and put gloves up and make this place just like a real operating room."

Soon the forceps were cool and he reached in with his two stumpy fingers and came out with the shiny tweezers and began transferring things from the hot water to the empty pot. He inserted the plunger in the syringe with the tweezers. He then placed the disk on the cooker and Tommie lighted a flame under it.

"The water's over there, Tommie."

Tommie took a bottle of distilled water from the cupboard and poured some into the disk. Then he spooned about a third of the powder from the tissue paper and carefully let it trickle over the edge of the spoon into the water. Hit-Man, armed with a syringe and needle, stirred the solution as it heated until the white substance dissolved in the water. He then drew the fluid into the syringe, smiled and said, "Who's first?"

"Me," Tommie said.

"I'll go next," I said.

"I guess that makes me third," Red Top said.

"Now listen, Hit-Man," Tommie said, a little nervous. "This stuff is straight, so take it easy."

"You doubt my ability, Tommie Tiger?"

"Oh, man, just give me the shot and don't start all them words." Tommie clamped his hand around the inside of his upper arm and opened and closed his fist a few times and the veins in his arm leaped up, almost as if they knew what was coming. Hit-Man made the thrust, found the vein and sent the joy juice pumping around Tommie's body.

Hit-Man changed the needle and came after me. I

did exactly what I had seen Tommie do—clamped down on my upper arm, opened and closed my fist a few times until the veins were setting up firm and ready. I felt the prick of the needle, the presence of something hot, almost stinging, heard Tommie say, "Oh, man, this shit is straight!" felt a little sick in the stomach for just an instant and then *wham!* I was floating, baby, and I didn't give a damn about anything that was going on around me. I closed my eyes and saw a world of sweet things. I saw thousands of wine bottles on sterling silver shelves. Millions of wine bottles. I took three and drank all three of them at the same time. It was the best wine I had ever tasted but it was all gone in one swallow. I walked back and forth in front of the shelves, taking bottles out, drinking them and throwing the bottles in the air, where they hung on the ceiling and sparkled with all the colors of this world and a few others. I drank and drank and drank.

I felt like I was getting a little sick and I opened my eyes and came back. I saw Hit-Man sitting on the Oriental rug with his legs crossed, swaying from side to side, humming along with the music that was coming from someplace in the room. His mouth was wide open and his eyes were closed. I wanted to laugh at him but I found myself trying to figure out how we had all gotten into the living room and onto the Oriental rug without my knowing it.

It wasn't really that important, so I closed my eyes and I went back to another world. This time I was sitting on a big rock looking down on six workmen who were taking a coffee break. A woman dressed in white approached and spoke in a soft voice that seemed to echo the minute it left her lips. "Won't one of you gentlemen help that poor old man with his telephone pole?" she said.

"What old guy you talking about, lady?" a man asked.

"The one with that enormous pole over his shoulder."

"Hey, lady," said another man, "you out of your mind? There ain't no man out there and there ain't no telephone pole nowhere in sight. Hey, you guys, I think this babe is a little sick."

"You mean none of you gentlemen can see him?"

"*No!*" they all shouted.

"But I can see him quite clearly, gentlemen. And he's getting so terribly old. Won't one of you please try to see him? He's right there. All you have to do is look and you can see him," she pleaded.

"Look, lady, you better get out of here before I call a cop," one of the men said. "You're too damn old to be out here soliciting on the corner."

The group laughed.

"But I can see him," she insisted.

"Well, how is it you can see him and we can't?"

"I don't know. I know I can see him, though."

"Okay, lady. Assuming he is out there, so damn what? What are you getting yourself all excited about? What is he to you, huh? Your boyfriend or something?"

"He's my son. Won't you please help him?"

"She's crazy! Get that babe out of here!" they shouted.

I opened my eyes and saw Tommie lying on his face. He wasn't breathing. "Hey, Hit-Man," I said. "What's wrong with Tommie?"

Hit-Man slapped Tommie in the face a few times, then took his foot and rolled him off the Oriental rug. "He's dead," he said.

"Really?"

"Dead, man. Real dead."

"Hey, Red Top," I said, "ain't that a drag. Tommie's dead. Ain't that a drag. From what?"

Hit-Man said, "A hot shot."

"Ain't that a drag. This cat had to go and die and try to spoil our fun."

Red Top smiled and shrugged his shoulders. Hit-Man didn't seem worried, either, so I forgot about old dead Tommie. He was a drag, anyway.

Early the next morning before the sun woke up the world, Red Top and I carried Tommie Murphy out the back door into the alley and dumped him in front of some cat's garage door about four blocks away. We didn't feel too bad about Tommie. We didn't feel at all bad about Tommie. He went out high like he wanted to, swinging from side to side in the silver chariot drawn by two high-stepping horses.

We still get the drags about as bad as ever, but we drink wine now. Wine is for civilized people and only savages use H.

little jo jo leaves us and we pledge vengeance

A month after the party, Luhester's youngest girl was badly scalded and had to be rushed to the hospital. The whole neighborhood worried as the child clung to the thin thread of life that remained. Doc called the county hospital every hour without fail and delivered the report to Silky Martin at the Cut-Rate Liquor Store, where we heard it.

Miss Joanne Joanne suffered as much as Luhester. She suffered more than Luhester. The baby had been named after her in keeping with an agreement the two ladies had made in Luhester's third month of pregnancy, and when Luhester went to the county hospital to deliver the child, Miss Joanne Joanne took charge of the other children. The day Luhester brought the baby home, Miss Joanne Joanne went shopping and bought everything the best-cared-for baby should have.

As little Jo Jo grew older, it was Miss Joanne Joanne who was seen pushing the carriage. And when she was sick, it was Miss Joanne Joanne who called the doctor or sat up with her through the night. Luhester had given birth to the child, but Miss Joanne Joanne had won the position of mother.

Little Jo Jo died after eight days of lingering and Miss Joanne Joanne refused to let the county bury her. That baby had the best funeral we've seen out this way since Preacher Pope Peterson died. We even had a high-class priest rubbing shoulders with two Baptist preachers. Red Top and I wore shirts and ties and white gloves and we rode in the big black Cadillac. (I remember thinking as we drove out to the cemetery to put the little child away that it was too bad people didn't rent those big pretty cars to bring their wives and babies home from the hospital instead of always taking the ride when it's finished, when there ain't no mo'.)

That night, after the funeral, we were all at Luhester's house feeling pretty bad about being alive and trying to drown our discomfort with a few fifths of gin (even Miss Joanne Joanne was drinking; she got drunk after a while and turned out to be a nice person), when Miss Joanne Joanne began mumbling something about the doctor at the county hospital. We heard the mumbling but it didn't make any sense to us because we weren't as drunk as she was. Everybody knows you can't understand a drunk until you're as drunk as he is.

By eleven o'clock we were all on a reasonably equal basis and Miss Joanne Joanne's mumbling began to make sense. "The doctor," she said. "The doctor said if they could only have gotten her sooner they probably could have saved her. He said maybe just a half hour would have made the difference. Now I ask you, why couldn't we get that baby there a half hour sooner?" She beat on the floor with her fists. "You tell me. Huh? Why couldn't we?"

The question seemed to hang in the air for the next half hour as we went on claiming closeness to the child.

"I remember," said Silky, "the first time she said dada. She was chewing on a rib in my place." He took out his handkerchief, blew his nose, wiped his eyes, blew his nose again and continued. "Every time Luhester used to bring her in, it just made the whole place kind of come to life."

I said, "Red Top and me were here when she first started eating from a spoon. I could get her to eat more for me than Luhester could because I used to make faces and she'd laugh."

"I was here when she started walking," Stick said. "Ain't that right, Luhester?"

Luhester nodded her head.

"Just a half hour," Miss Joanne Joanne said. "Just one half hour. That's all we needed. Just one god-damned half hour."

Fat Man staggered through the door, shouting. "The white man's gone too damn far this time. God's gonna make him pay for this."

We pulled Fat Man down to the floor with us and he told us his story. "I was drinking in the back of Doc's store," he said. "And Roosevelt Washington came down the alley asking me how was Luhester's baby. So I told him she was dead. He said he wasn't surprised. So I asks him what he means. He says he was in South Side getting sewed up from where Jellie had cut him in a fight, when the nurse brought the baby in, put it on the table and left her there for about forty-five minutes before the police came and took her to the county. He says if he hadn't had no money on him they wouldn't have sewed him up. He says the first thing they asked him was if he had any money and when he pulled out his roll they took what they wanted and started sewing him up."

The room was quiet for the first time in hours. It was sobering-up time.

Miss Joanne Joanne turned to Cadillac Bill and said in an angry voice, "Bill, you drove them there. I know you had some money."

"Wait a minute," Cadillac Bill pleaded. "I just drove. I let Doc and Luhester out. They rushed the baby in and I went on and parked the car. When I got there, they was sittin' in the waitin' room and I asked Luhester if they was takin' care of the baby and she said they sure was."

"Is that right, Doc?" Miss Joanne Joanne demanded.

"That's right," Doc said nervously. "They didn't even ask us if we had no money. We took the baby in and I said to the nurse to please save our baby. She taken the baby and went through them swingin' doors and we didn't even see her for fifteen or twenty minutes and then all she did was come out and look down her big stuck-up white nose at us."

Miss Joanne Joanne screamed. "We'll sue the chalk-face bastards for every penny they've got."

"God's gonna make the white man pay this time," Fat Man said.

"No he ain't," Doc said. "He's got too much to do. He ain't gonna have to make 'em pay. I'm gonna make 'em pay myself."

"You and me," Cadillac Bill said. "We'll make 'em pay."

Doc stood up, tripped over me, stumbled into the wall, righted himself and said, "We gonna burn it down. We gonna burn that white man's hospital to a crisp. That's the way to get even with the bastards. You with me, Cadillac?"

"I'm with you."

"So am I," Fat Man said. "As soon as I have another drink of this gin."

It was a good idea so we all drank to it. And then we drank to burning the doctors and nurses. And when we finished drinking to that, we drank to burning the mayor, city hall and all the white people in the world. And pretty soon we forgot what we were supposed to be drinking to and began drinking to the bottles we had emptied. After all, it *was* awfully good gin.

johnnie sweepstakes, a gambling man

Johnnie Sweepstakes left Mississippi at the age of fifteen with his cousin, who was coming to Chicago to sell his ten-year-old car, double his money and buy a policy wheel. Just outside of Chicago they passed a racetrack, made a U-turn and arrived inside the track in time to cheer the ponies in the home stretch of the sixth race. Johnnie borrowed two dollars from his cousin and bet it on a horse called Southern Lady in the seventh race. Of course Southern Lady won and paid sixteen-to-one and Johnnie Sweepstakes was hooked for life.

When they arrived at their destination they stopped at the Cut-Rate to celebrate their joyous day with the comfort given by a bottle of beer and a shot of gin. Inside the bar there was an even bigger celebration going on. One of the local gentlemen had hit the numbers that day for a grand total of two hundred dollars and was in the bar drinking his winnings in the form of the most expensive Scotch he could buy.

Johnnie Sweepstakes had never played policy before, but it seemed like a good idea, and, of course, he was hooked from the start. He bet the numbers every day for the next fifteen years. He had not yet hit, but it was only twenty-five or fifty cents a day so he never missed it. Besides, he knew someday he'd hit big and then he was on the way up.

One form of entertainment leads to another and Johnnie could not be whole until he had almost mastered blackjack and poker; and even then there was something missing in his life, some little fragment to pull all the loose pieces together. And then one day after years of searching he found it. He was clearing away the dishes at the restaurant where he worked as a busboy when he heard two men discussing the coming Irish Sweepstakes, the grandest race in the world. And from that day on he dreamed of winning the real race.

It wasn't as if he were wishing for someone to come along and give him a tip; it wasn't as if he wanted to be lucky just once; it was a fact—he was destined to win the Irish Sweepstakes and he let everyone know it.

I don't know who first called him Johnnie Sweepstakes and I don't remember with certainty when the name began to stick with him, but I think it happened sometime during the year he lost one week's salary on the grand race. Like I said, he knew he was destined to win, but since he didn't know when he would win, he had to continue looking forward to the next year. He was always preparing for the next year because that was the big one and the prizes would be greater than ever.

It never seemed fair to me that one man should lose so much when he had everything going for him. He couldn't win. It just wasn't possible for him to win at anything. He lost at policy, at horses, at blackjack, at poker and even at matching and pitching pennies with the kids. Another person might have given it up for honest savings in a bank, but not Johnnie Sweepstakes—never! Providence had willed that he would win the grand race and get back every penny plus; so until that time came, he was going to enjoy the sheer sport of it all, no matter how much it would cost him.

Well, one day luck finally came to Johnnie Sweepstakes in the form of ten-one-nine and a twenty-five-cent policy bet. The numbers were the first letters of his nickname and that surely had to be a good omen.

Johnnie had a room in the hotel on the second floor just off the stairway. Red Top and I returned home from spending a day in the Street, and could hear the noise as we entered the building. "Johnnie," someone shouted over the crowd. "You the luckiest stud in Chicago."

I grabbed Red Top's arm. "Red Top, the Sweepstakes is next month, ain't it?"

"Yeah. That's a long way off. How the hell can he be lucky? He ain't never won nothin'."

We hurried up the stairs and saw a room full of bottles held by hands that belonged to bodies that belonged to people—everyone had a fifth.

Johnnie called to us: "Hey, man, you cats come on in and grab whatsoever you wants. Johnnie Sweepstakes is buyin' the way real gamblers buy. Ain't that right, baby?" he said to a woman who was hanging around his waist. She nodded and squeezed tighter.

"Sweepstakes," I said. "For what, man? For what?"

"For ten-one-nine, man. For ten-one-nine to the tune of two thousand little dark greens. I'm gonna break the bank tomorrow. Like I been tellin' you, man, I'm the luckiest stud in the world. It just takes a little time. That's all. It just takes a little time and patience." He disappeared into the crowd, with the young lady hanging on.

Red Top and I each took a bottle of Scotch and joined the party. I think we were both relieved to know that he hadn't won the Irish Sweepstakes.

The party lasted all night and Johnnie called for more liquor at twelve o'clock, at two o'clock, at three o'clock, at four o'clock and at five o'clock. The room was much too small so eventually the party extended to every room on the second floor and then down to the first floor. Pete up at the Cut-Rate was giving Johnnie a fair cut in price, but the liquor bill still climbed to five hundred dollars. But that was nothing to Johnnie because he was entertaining like a real gambler should.

Red Top and I tried to go to bed at four o'clock but our beds were in use, so we went downstairs and partied in the street with others who had come outside to breathe. We were in front of the hotel so we didn't see the accident.

I was told (by someone who was sober enough to know) that Johnnie Sweepstakes was bragging about his ability to pick numbers and laughing about the sickening expression on the face of the payoff man, and laughed so hard he had to sit down. He sat on the windowsill, forgot it was summer and the window was up, and fell out. Judging from the way he was screaming, his leg must have been broken.

The ambulance came. The attendant and driver splinted the leg and rolled him into their white hearse. The attendant didn't like the size of the crowd and wanted to leave. You see, the driver had accepted a bottle and was doing his best to catch up with us. The attendant had refused at least five offers and was becoming irritated with his partner. Finally he shouted to him, "C'mon, Bill. Let's get this guy to the county so we can go home."

Johnnie Sweepstakes heard him and screamed, "Don't y'all take me to no county hospital. I got money. You hear me! I got money. Take me to a *private* hospital." He fumbled through a fistful of money. "Here," he said, "take this." He tossed two ten-dollar bills onto the front seat. "Take me to a private hospital. One of them rich white hospitals. And I wants to pay for this here ambulance ride, too. I'm a gamblin' man. I got plenty of money."

Johnnie Sweepstakes was hospitalized for six weeks with a fractured femur. It took every penny he had left to pay the hospital bill, but that didn't matter to Johnnie Sweepstakes, because he was a gambling man.

That year he did not win the Irish Sweepstakes but he didn't lose heart; he was positive that the coming year would be the one for him. It had to be—all the signs pointed to it.

build me a church

Chicago is divided into a series of neighborhoods where people of like backgrounds gather together to preserve their customs. These neighborhoods are like isolated villages and life within them is so complete that a person could conceivably live in an area of two or three square miles and never have reason to step over the boundary line.

Once a year each neighborhood has a parade of some kind that symbolizes everything its inhabitants believe in. The Irish import a dignitary from Ireland; the Chinese line the walks with people dressed in their native garb; the Spanish file through the streets with a crucifix in the lead on their way to a solemn high mass. Every neighborhood has some cause for a parade at least once a year. In addition to these private affairs spotting the city from time to time, the downtown businessmen of the Chicago Chamber of Commerce manage to provide five or six parades a year for the benefit of the entire city.

Now all of these parades could pass through our little World of Nothing at the same time and they couldn't begin to generate the excitement that Preacher Gibson does when he brings his tent church to the vacant lot at the end of the block every year after the Fourth of July. It's probably the smallest parade in the world, but it's our kind of parade, geared to stir our emotions and send us scurrying to the vacant lot to get the tent up.

Preacher Gibson is obviously a man of means, but shrewd enough to travel light. On the day of the parade Sister Grace can be heard warming up on her bass drum one hour after the sun comes up. Boom-boom. Boom-boom. Boom-boom. The drum works like the jungle telegraph system and by nine o'clock the street is filled with children screaming for the most sensational parade of the year.

At exactly nine-fifteen sharp Sister Grace really goes to work on the bass drum. Boom, boom-boom, boom, boom-boom. And all the time she's screaming one hymn after another. I've never been able to understand a word she says, but I know she's saying something good because of the way she holds her head back and shakes it from side to side, her hair plastered down so tight that not one strand is disturbed. She's perfect for leading the parade.

Following Sister Grace are two neighborhood sisters who volunteered for the position of banner carriers. They hold the banner high and strut and smile and shake their big fat asses all over the place. The banner is a dirty sheet, worn through years of service, upon which the words "GOD MOVES" have been rather unprofessionally printed in huge red letters. That is the name of the church. These are really good sisters and they are allowed to wear long white dresses and sit in the front row of the church, provided, of course, they are able to get in.

About twenty feet behind the banner-carrying sisters comes a strikingly attired figure, Preacher Gibson. He's a big man, six feet three inches tall, two hundred eighty pounds of sculptured ebony with a three-inch pile of greasy black hair that shines and captures the eyes of all the women. He moves catlike down the street in a pair of gold shoes, gold socks, a gold suit, shirt and tie, and he wears two thick gold rings on his thumbs—and he blows a slide trombone! He brings up the rear of the parade and brings us up with him. He blows eight bars, then he whirls in the middle of the street and shouts a sermon in two sentences to one side of the street: "God moves. I come to move you." Then he blows four bars, jumps eight feet off the ground, spins in the air, kicks his feet out, screams like a million seagulls, hits the ground shaking his head, falls to his knees, points his shiny trombone at the people on the other side of the street and says, "You're all dead. I come to give you life." Then he walks half of the block on his knees blowing his head off, pulls the trombone away from his lips, screams, does a somersault, springs to his feet and runs to the front of the parade, whirling the instrument over his head, panting and sweating. When he reaches the head of the parade, he stands with his legs apart and vibrates himself into a trance. He closes his eyes and shouts, "God moves! Build me a church!" And falls *flat* on his back.

And at the sound of these words two hundred children race into the vacant lot; men and women scream and cry and fall out on the street and roll in the dirt and let go of everything. People pour into the vacant lot and the church goes up in a matter of minutes. Preacher Gibson doesn't see it until that night, however, because he has to be carried away to his room, just like every year after his soul-stirring performance, to rest up for the coming night.

Once a year is enough.

Red Top and Frenchy Coolbreeze couldn't stay away from the church—Red Top because he was sharing Sister Grace with Preacher Gibson and Frenchy Coolbreeze because he was having a ball playing his French horn with the swinging preacher. I refused to go because I had seen it in years past and I knew what he'd do to me—he'd get all of my money just like he always did. I knew what he was going to do. He was going to preach and scream and shout and jump and play his trombone until he had drained the people of all of their money and then he would send word around that he was leaving, but that he wanted everyone to come to the last meeting and not to give him any money because, even though he was poor, God would see to it that he managed to survive. And on that last night people would not bring money, but they would bring food; they would bring enough food to feed the Preacher and Sister Grace for six months. And then Preacher Gibson would get them all to help dismantle the church and pack it in his truck along with the food and then he would be gone. No, I knew what was going to happen and I stayed away from the place because I wasn't going to give him a damn cent.

As it turned out, Red Top gave him enough money for both of us. And as if that wasn't bad enough, then he started working for the guy and following him around and eventually driving him around town in Frenchy's car. While they were out driving, Frenchy learned a few things about life from Sister Grace.

place of peace closes and all doors open

I remember last year they came around, swarms of them: building inspectors, fire inspectors, plumbing inspectors, electrical inspectors—the works. They came around every day for a week or so and then we didn't see them again until the first of this month. And now they've come back with the police and put us all out. Just like that. They put us out of our home. All right, so it was a firetrap; so it did have substandard partitions or whatever you call them; so there weren't enough exits; so the plumbing was bad; so the wiring was defective—it was still our home. They put us out in the street and boarded the damn place up.

The owners are the ones they should have put out—they should have put them right out of business. They should, but they say they can't find them. Now you tell me how a man or a group of men can have a building and make money on it for all of these years and nobody knows who he or they are? It just doesn't sound right to me. The whole thing stinks.

We didn't know what to do. Luhester took some of us in and put us up in her basement. Reverend Edwards took a bunch in his church and Father Lane put the rest in his gymnasium. Thank God for Reverend Edwards, Luhester and Father Lane. Thank God for all the reverends and priests and nice ladies with babies.

But if they hadn't put us out of there, the place never would have burned down. If we had still been living there, everything would have been all right. The only reason the kids started the fire was because there was nobody in the building. And wouldn't you know it, the Place of Peace went out like a screaming giant. We had the biggest fire this part of the city has ever seen. There were fire engines all around the block. There were so many firemen that most of them just stood around looking at the fire and shouting at the kids who were getting in the way.

The really surprising thing about the fire is that no

one was injured and the buildings on either side received only slight damage and most of that from the water the firemen put on them.

Now I'm not superstitious, but if you think about it awhile it does seem strange that the fire didn't spread to the other buildings. The flames just went *straight* up and didn't bother anything else. It seems like the Place of Peace got angry because they took its people away, and just burned itself right down to the ashes. That shows you what the old Place of Peace thought of the city officials. I wonder what's going to grow from the ashes?

red top travels on

Red Top is gone. He's moved. He's left. Red Top is traveling in search of a light. I can't lean on him anymore. He and Frenchy Coolbreeze packed their bags and drove away to some other city with the tent church. I think they are going south for the winter.

He didn't even say good-bye. He couldn't look me in the eye and say good-bye. We could have shaken hands, slapped each other on the back and made a few jokes about the church. No—that wouldn't have worked. He doesn't like jokes about the church anymore. But he did leave me the note and I understand why he left. It's a short note, but I get the message.

> Can't make it this way. Found something that gives my life meaning and I couldn't stand to lose it. Hope you find it, too. See you next year. To the glory of God. I remain.

I don't know what to think or how to feel about it other than a deep sense of loneliness and perhaps even rejection. But what the hell, we were only roommates. That's true. That's very true. But still . . . you get used to being around a person: doing silly things, going to the usual places, sort of leaning on each other as you walk down the street fighting your way through the world together, each being only one-half of the whole, and then one half finds the other half of itself gone. I think if I weren't living in Luhester's basement with the people around me every minute of the day—yes, I think I might kill myself. I don't think there's much hope for me just now. Right now the only feeling I have is that Red Top is dead and I am half dead.

I just don't know what I'm going to do. I know I'm going to miss the old Place of Peace, though. It seems like everything died at about the same time: Red Top is lost to God's world, the hotel is lost to the wrecking crew's world and I'm just lost. And judging from the way my mind has been clicking off ideas lately, I'm afraid I'm going to be lost to conformity. I don't like the idea at all, but it looks like there's going to have to be a job in the making for me. Conformity—that's what it will be. I'll be punching a clock like the rest of the look-alikes. Up in the morning, eight on the job, home in the evening and not too much drinking because there will always be tomorrow morning staring me in the face.

Chained! That's what I'll be. I'll be chained just like the rest—meeting payments for all kinds of shit I don't really need, shaving and changing clothes and keeping my shoes shined and taking girls out and spending money on them because when you've got a job people expect you to act a certain way and they just don't give you a chance to be yourself. I don't like it at all, dammit! But that's the way I'll have to be because there's nothing left here.

My World of Nothing is gone. It's disappeared. It's not the same. I can't see it like I used to. I can't see it at all, so it must be gone. The Street isn't even the same. The lights are dim; they're not nearly as bright as they used to be. The elevated doesn't even make the same kind of noise it used to. It's all changed now. That damn Peter even raised the price on the wine down at the Cut-Rate. They're organizing against us. A man's got to have a job even to buy a pint of wine now. As far as I'm concerned, they can have the place. Anybody who wants it can have it, because I'm leaving. As far as I'm concerned, this damn place doesn't exist—I just erased it from my mind.

from half to whole

Guess what? I found another roommate. Yeah. This guy is great. He's even more fun than Red Top. I had to write about this day because it's been my day of salvation. My new roommate is sleeping in a stuffed chair in my apartment (one of the things I bought when I started working many months ago), and I thought I'd better get my notebook out of the trunk and record this day because I've got the feeling that I won't be writing much longer. No need to—I won't be alone now, not ever, and I've changed somewhat through my experiences of conformity over the long months. This guy is just like me: Buy what you want and beg what you need. It's great to meet someone who is alive. Oh, God, it feels good to be alive again. To be free to be alive again.

I left my job at the parking lot downtown at five o'clock today and picked up a girl at the telephone company. I had made a date with her at noon to take her to dinner and out for a few drinks and then up to my place. We had dinner at one of those $1.19 steak houses (pretty good steaks for a dollar nineteen) and she wanted to see something different so we got on the elevated and rode out to the World of Nothing and started bar-hopping.

We passed Marovitz's place and there was this guy outside who walked up to me and said, "Hey, man, can you give me any help?"

The young lady with me cringed because he did look pretty dirty and ragged.

"What kind of help do you mean?" I asked.

She tugged at my sleeve. "Give him the money and let's get out of here."

"Anything you can spare, man. I haven't eaten in two days."

"Are you puttin' me on, man? Are you really hungry or are you stacking it up for a bottle of blood?"

"Wine? Hell no, man, I'm hungry. I got my wine already. I want some food now." He reached in his back pocket and came out with a pint of wine.

That was the most refreshing experience of my new life. A man after my own heart. And he had guts enough to stand up and say it. I took him by the arm. "Come on, man," I said. "You I'll buy dinner for."

"You're not going to take him with us?" my date asked.

"That's right."

"But look at him."

"So he's dirty. You said you wanted to come down here. Well, here we are. And besides, any man that talks like him must be all right." The three of us started down the street together heading for Silky Martin's. When we got there this guy goes into the washroom, washes his face and hands, takes a sip of his wine, comes back and even says grace before he eats the ribs.

Now I ask you: Isn't that something great? Washed and even said a grace! A guy like this makes you feel proud that you can help him out.

This guy is funny, too. He knows a million jokes. And he's been all over the country. He used to spend the summers in New York and then work his way across the country to get to California just about the time it gets cold back here. I don't know too much about him yet, except that he's a great talker and seems a little mixed up like most people. And he really needs somebody to lean on for a while and he'll be all right. He talks all the time. And you know, he even makes sense. Even my girl liked him after she got to know him a little better.

So I suggested to him that he come to my pad and spend a few days until he got himself together. He thought I was a little strange at first, but when I explained to him that I had shared a place with a guy for a couple of years and wasn't used to being alone, he understood. I don't blame him for not trusting me. Most people don't really want to help you. They just want to take for themselves. I was so happy to meet somebody like him in this world that I practically picked him up and carried him to the apartment. He agreed, and there he is, half in the chair, half out of it, and here I am and here we are, brothers of our way of life.

70 71 72 73 10 9 8 7 6 5 4 3 2 1